The Haunted House Project

The Haunted House Project

Tricia Clasen

Sky Pony Press
New York

Sky Pony Press books may be purchased in bulk at special discounts for sales promotion, corporate gifts, fund-raising, or educational purposes. Special editions can also be created to specifications. For details, contact the Special Sales Department, Sky Pony Press, 307 West 36th Street, 11th Floor, New York, NY 10018 or info@skyhorsepublishing.com.

Sky Pony® is a registered trademark of Skyhorse Publishing, Inc.®, a Delaware corporation.

Visit our website at www.skyponypress.com.

10 9 8 7 6 5 4 3 2 1

Library of Congress Cataloging-in-Publication Data is available on file.

Cover design by Georgia Morrissey
Cover illustration credit: Sean Hayden

Print ISBN: 978-1-5107-0712-2
Ebook ISBN: 978-1-5107-0713-9

Printed in the United States of America

Interior design by Joshua Barnaby

For Grace and Faith.

Because raising you to follow your dreams reminded me of my own.

Chapter One

I knock on the door three times and then lean in close, listening for the rustle of the bedspread or the thud of feet hitting the floor. I don't hear anything, so I crack the door and stick my head inside.

"Time to get up, Paige," I call out.

My sister greets me with a groan. "Go away, Andie." She throws the covers off, though, so I take that as a good sign. I back away, leaving the door open.

Even though she's seventeen and I'm thirteen, I'm always the one to make sure she's up. It didn't used to be that way. She used to beat me out the door every morning with her chestnut hair blown dry and her lips perfectly glossed. She would breeze past me in the kitchen and pat me on the head while I shoveled eggs into my mouth. Now she stumbles through mornings, grabbing whatever jeans lie on the floor by her bed and pulling her hair into a ponytail.

Then again, lots of things changed this year.

I stop outside my dad's bedroom door. Sometimes I think I can still smell her here. Right now, I'd love even a hint of the stuff she used to spritz that made her smell like a tropical island. I inhale deeply. Nothing. It's probably for the best. Even if I could catch a whiff, I know I'd be imagining things. Because she's gone.

They say she didn't know what hit her. No pain. No life flashing before her eyes. Just here, then gone. They say that was for the best. I'm not so sure. My mom liked to be in control. I sort of think she would have wanted a chance to argue her way out of what was coming. Not that you can talk to a semi speeding toward you at seventy miles an hour. Still, if anyone could, it would have been her.

I can almost hear her: "What do you think you're doing? Oh no, you don't get to just plow into me like that. I have way too much to do. Move. Now. Go." It would be like when she used to rush us out the door in the morning. I never thought I'd miss that. Or the yelling. But I'd give anything for just one "Andie, hurry up!" or even a "Don't you dare give me that attitude. Get in the car. Move. Now. Go."

Then again, maybe if she'd known she was about to die, it wouldn't have been fair, because her last thought would have been about the storm that would brew in her wake and how it would rain down all kinds of stink on my life. She wouldn't have wanted that.

I don't bother knocking on my dad's door. There's only a fifty-fifty chance he's in there at all, and even if he is, he wouldn't wake up if I played the drums next to his bed. He was always a sound sleeper, but late nights at the casino and whatever he drowns himself in besides grief knock him out for the long haul. Paige and I used to try harder—we didn't want him to be late to work, or worse yet miss it altogether. I gave up after he lost the second job. I've got enough to deal with.

It doesn't take me long to get ready because I cut my hair short a couple of months ago. It's not as brown as Paige's, and I think it probably looked better long. But this is easy, just like the jeans and plain gray T-shirt I've thrown on. And it gives me time for one last story before breakfast.

Ghost stories have kind of always been my thing. That sounds weird, more like silly ghost stories, Goosebumps-type stuff or the ones about the ghost cat who solves mysteries. But I've moved on. My new hobby is reading stories about paranormal activity. I've read like a gazillion that I've found on the web. Most of them are stupid and really fake, but I can't stop reading.

I skim quickly through the list of entries on a message board. "My Experience with Ouija." Lots of those on here. "The Devil May Have Called Me." I roll my eyes at that one.

Then I stop breathing for a second and my heart races.

My hand shakes a little when I click on "Visit from My Mother?"

Last night, I was watching some old home movies with my son. I wanted him to see the videos of my mom, and the first one up was from a Halloween when I was about eleven. I was all dressed up as a witch, begging my mom to hurry up so we could go trick-or-treating. We watched as the doorbell rang, and she gave some little girls in princess costumes some candy. I paused the video to tell my son about how my mom had made the witch costume for me. Suddenly, our doorbell rang. I ran to the front door. Nothing there. No kids running away or bags of poop. Chills ran down my arms. I went back to the family room and pressed play. The video skipped ahead to us out walking around the neighborhood. The camera followed me up a driveway while I pressed a neighbor's doorbell. I yelled out, "Trick or treat!" My mom waved to the neighbor. Then, our doorbell rang again.

My mother's been dead for over ten years, but I think she may have wanted us to know she was here. Who knows?

It's a stupid story. Still, I'm jealous. I'd give anything for one phantom doorbell ring. I close the page in frustration and head downstairs.

In the kitchen, I open and shut every cupboard a few times. I guess I could have canned peas for breakfast. But besides the fact that peas make me gag, I can't imagine how old they are. There haven't been many vegetables in the house lately. I pull a bag out of the bread box and find a semi-crushed hunk of white bread, along with the heel. I open the bag and sniff. They still smell good. I pop them both in the toaster, then open the fridge and dig around for some butter. No luck, but there's enough jelly to cover at least one of the pieces. And, surprisingly, there's milk. But when I take a whiff of that, the sour stings my nostrils. I hold my breath as I dump the chunky milk down the sink.

Paige slinks into the kitchen, her eyes weighed down by sleep and sadness that won't ever go away. She rests her elbow on the table and leans her face against one hand. I toss her a piece of toast, and she bites immediately.

I approach her slowly, like she's a stray dog. She's pretty tame, but you never know what will set her off. "Um, Paige, my lunch account at school is empty. They say they sent a note. I can't get hot lunch until I put more money in."

She sighs and rubs the back of her head with her hand. "I don't have anything. Not until Friday when I get paid." She doesn't say anything else, but I know what's she's thinking. Not even then, really, if she puts gas in her car and pays the electric company something. I saw the big red letters on the front of the envelope. It's not her fault. I know that, but I'm still mad.

"Ugh. What I am supposed to eat? There's nothing here. What is wrong with everyone in this house?" I stomp over to the sink and run the water, trying to rinse the room of the smell that lingers from the milk. But that's not really the stink I want to get rid of.

And now I'm mad at myself, too. Paige doesn't need me acting like a brat.

"I'm sorry, Andie," she says. Her voice comes out cracked. "I'll try to get another shift this week."

I glance at the empty bread bag. I shouldn't have had the toast. Bread and jelly would have been easier to take for lunch than canned peas.

"Do you think—" I pause. We try not to talk about Dad. "Well, do you think he's got any money?"

She shrugs. "You want to wake him up to find out?"

I close my eyes and remember how we used to pile on Mom and Dad's bed on Sundays, giggling and bouncing. Dad would pretend to stay asleep, fake snoring, until he'd jump up and tickle us. Now if we try to wake him up, he either growls, swears, or throws a shoe at the door. Besides, even if he had money, he's probably spent it. I've heard him and Paige fighting about him throwing money away at the casino. Mom's money. There wasn't that much. He paid off the house with some, which is good because at least they can't take that away. If we lost the house, there'd never be a chance I could smell her again. There's some money in two special accounts—one for Paige and one for me—but we can't get it until we're eighteen. Paige only has to wait four more months, and I'm a little worried that as soon as that day comes, she'll be gone.

So I try not to bug her too much.

"I guess not."

"I'll go check all my jeans to see if I have enough change so you can get something in the cafeteria."

I shake my head. "Never mind. I'll figure out something."

"Sorry," she says again.

I turn away so she can't see my tears. It's not fair. For her or for me. I take a breath and blink to clear my eyes. My mom always said, "Crying will make you feel better, but it doesn't solve anything." My mom was big on solutions.

I wish she was big on doorbells, too.

Chapter Two

At school, the morning drags. By second period, my stomach twists and groans, and my head pounds. My eyelids droop as Mr. Jackson writes on the board. I can't say I love pre-algebra, but usually I can at least follow along. Today, the numbers and letters blur together, and I let my head rest on my desk. Someone brushes me as they walk past my desk. I jump and wipe a bit of drool off my chin. I look around quickly to see if anyone has noticed, but they're all rushing out of the room without looking back. Ugh, class is already over.

Then I catch Mr. Jackson's eye, and he raises an eyebrow.

I shrug and sigh.

"That's twice this week, Andie."

"I know. I'm sorry."

My stomach lets out one of those long slow grumbles right at that moment.

"I guess you'd better get to lunch."

"Yeah." I nod, but I can't look at him.

Mr. Jackson's voice gets quieter. "Andie, is everything okay?"

I never know how to answer a question like that. I mean, no, it's not. It's never going to be okay again. But that's not what people want to hear. Like Paige says, sometimes telling the truth about how you feel is just not worth it.

I shrug. "Are my grades bad?"

"No, not really. You're doing fine. It's just that . . . well, just let me know if you need anything, okay?"

"Okay." That's another one of those statements that I don't know what to do with. What can people do? Can they bring my mom back? Can they get my dad to go to work every day? Do they really expect me to ask for groceries?

I fake a smile, because I've learned that makes people feel better.

Lunch is better than I expect.

"Are you on a diet?" Leah asks. She's got a carrot hanging out of her mouth and she talks around it as she reaches up and pulls her black hair into a bun.

I shake my head. "Grocery day."

Three heads turn in my direction. I suspect they know things aren't great, but we all pretend that it's just another year. Another day. No one died. No one's dad gambles away all the money. No one only has a can of peas in the house to eat. They try to be supportive, but they don't understand at all. Paige says people expect you to stop talking about it after a while, and I think she's right. Like, in the beginning they would listen and give me hugs, but they don't want to see me cry when they're thinking about quizzes and school dances. It's better for them when I'm just the same old Andie. Carefree. Funny. The Andie who sticks celery sticks up her nose and wears lime-green shirts and big bows in her hair.

Without saying anything, food suddenly comes my way.

"Yuck, why does my mom keep putting grapes in my lunch? She knows I can't stand them." Leah holds the bag out to me. Her blue eyes sparkle and her pink lips are pursed together in a tight smile. I ignore the pang in my heart when she mentions her mom and reach for the grapes.

A few minutes later, Becki leans back. "I've been such a pig lately. I better not touch these cookies." She pushes them toward me. Lately, she's always complaining about being too big. The problem is she's the tallest girl in class, so she's always going to be bigger than the rest of us. Of course, Becki can't just let me eat the cookies without a dig. Lately, there are lots of digs. "You never have to worry about weight since you don't have to put on a cheerleading uniform."

I ignore the tone that says I'm not as great as she is, because I want the cookies. Still, Becki is one more thing that changed this year that I sure wish hadn't. I glance around to see if anyone else noticed her comment, but everyone's focused on their food. Kind of like me and no food, we pretend Becki didn't get meaner after her parents announced they were getting a divorce. The cookies rock, though. Soft chocolate chip, my absolute favorite.

We've all been friends pretty much forever. Becki and Leah took dance lessons together when they were only three. I met Leah in preschool, but all of us really got close when we had to do a Thanksgiving play together in second grade. We were cast as Pilgrims One through Four. I was Pilgrim Two. With three lines, Gisela spoke the most. That meant we all did a lot of waiting around at rehearsal. And we had a blast together. Mr. Rushall, the music teacher, yelled at us almost every day for giggling too loud. That was the way it always was with us. We had so much fun together even though we're all pretty different from each other. Since starting middle school, the differences are standing out more. Leah's so busy she doesn't always have time to breathe, let alone talk to anyone. These days Becki really worries about what everyone else thinks all the time, especially the other cheerleaders. Gisela's the constant—she hasn't changed as much.

I'm lost in thought when she hands me her bottle of water. "I'm going to grab a juice instead," she says before standing up and heading back to the à la carte line.

I can't say I'll walk out of the cafeteria full, but at least my belly won't attack me from the inside out. I appreciate the snacks, but sometimes this is lonely. I know my friends don't really understand how bad things are at our house. And they've all got problems, too. Gisela's parents don't have "papers," as she calls them. I know she worries about that, and their English isn't so great, so she has to help them translate a lot, too. Becki's parents split up just over a year ago. She brags about it at Christmas when she gets double the presents, but I know it still bothers her, and she hates dividing her time. Leah, well, her life is pretty good. Leah's never really had anything bad happen; she's just caught up in her own very busy and very organized world most of the time.

"So, I'm calling for a sleepover Friday," Becki says, my thoughts interrupted once again. "I'll be at my dad's house and he won't care." I nod immediately, wishing it wasn't only Wednesday. I love sleepovers. Sleepovers are all about happy families, lots of snacks, and usually pizza. And all I have to do in exchange is pretend to be happy for a few hours. At this point I'm pretty good at faking it.

Leah shakes her head. "Can't. I have to study for Battle of the Books, and I've got soccer Saturday morning." I sink a little.

If Gisela can't go either, maybe Becki won't want just me to come. I'm not even sure I'd want to go. Gisela tilts her head. "I have to check with my parents. One of my cousins is having a birthday party, but I think it's on Saturday afternoon, so it should be okay."

"Cool," Becki says. "Andie, need my dad to call yours?"

My face crinkles up as I try to figure out why her dad would want to talk to mine, but then I remember that my mom always insisted on talking directly with parents before playdates and sleepovers. That's what moms do, but then again, mine really did like to be in control. She always had to know where we were.

"Nah," I choke out. Then I add a lie. "I'll talk to him tonight."

After lunch we scatter in different directions. Unfortunately, our class schedules don't overlap much this year. It stinks, especially for Becki, who really hates going to class by herself. "Why couldn't any of you take choir? Just one of you!"

Leah giggles. "Why couldn't any of you be on the quiz bowl team?"

Becki rolls her eyes. "Andie, you've got it the worst. I can't believe you got stuck with Isaiah Hardy as a science partner. He's so weird."

They all groan and nod. Isaiah's weirdness seems to be the one thing everyone can agree on.

I mean, yeah, about once a week, he wears a bow tie to school. The other days he's usually in a T-shirt with some dorky science saying on it, like the one that says, NEVER TRUST AN ATOM; THEY MAKE UP EVERYTHING. Okay fine, that one makes me giggle. But does he have to wave his geek flag so high with that blue TARDIS shirt? Don't even get me started on those glasses he wears that take up half his face. Still, I don't mind him. And it's not just because he's always got the right answers. He leaves me alone more than anyone else, and he doesn't act any different around me now.

I get to science early, and since I've got a few minutes before people start showing up, I pull out a book. No, not one of my textbooks, but the paperback I checked out of the library a couple days ago.

I'm so immersed in the book that I don't notice the other kids start to file in until someone yanks it out of my hand.

"*The Ghosts of Avalon Lake*," Isaiah reads, examining the cover, then flips through some pages. "Why do you read this junk?"

Isaiah lacks some of the filters that other people have. The ones that tell you what you should and shouldn't say.

"I don't know. I like it. Give it back," I say, reaching for the book. It's bow tie day, and today's is bright yellow, and it stands out against the white button-down shirt and his dark skin. It's a little crooked.

Isaiah ignores me and continues flipping through the pages. He shakes his head while he skims, and I notice his Afro is also a bit uneven, kind of crooked, like his tie. "Have you always liked ghost stories?"

"Pretty much." I sit up and my fists clench. It's true. I've always loved scary camp stories and Goosebumps, once I discovered them, and I even love cheesy horror movies. Sometimes on the weekend, Paige lets me stay up and watch them with her. It used to freak my mom out and she would turn the TV off if she thought a movie might give me night- mares. She didn't stop me from reading any books, though.

"Do you believe in ghosts?"

The question slaps me across the face in a way I don't expect. Maybe because I've been asking myself the same question for months now. I didn't used to. I read books and watched movies, but it was all fun and games. Scary for the rush. But no, back then I didn't think ghosts were real.

"I'm not sure."

It's not so much that my opinion has changed; it's just that I really like the idea that she might be around somewhere, watching out for me.

He nods slowly as he stares at me. Sometimes I think he gets me more than anyone else.

"Well, your book choices are garbage," he says, tossing the paperback in my direction.

After class starts, Isaiah turns toward the front of the room and gives all his attention to the teacher. After about twenty minutes of being forced to pretend that chemical bonds are exciting, the teacher announces that we have the rest of the class to work on our projects. We're supposed to be learning about the scientific method. So, we have to do background research on a science topic, plus do our own simple experiment where we create a hypothesis and figure out the variables. Isaiah and I have been brainstorming for a week, and we still haven't decided what we're going to research.

"Are you into the environment?"

"Huh?" I ask.

"You know, like the ozone layer, or recycling."

"We used to compost," I say too quickly. *Please don't ask me why we stopped.* His eyes narrow, but he doesn't say anything else about it.

"Space?"

I crinkle my nose and shake my head.

"Oceans?"

I shrug.

"Ghosts?"

My mouth drops, and I punch him in the arm. I'm so mad I wish I could I have hit his face instead.

"What?" he asks.

"Don't make fun of me."

"I'm not. I mean it. We could study paranormal activity."

"For science?"

"Sure, why not?"

My heart rate picks up and I sit a little straighter.

I open my notebook and start writing. We talk fast, and I can barely keep up with my notes. The ideas are flowing. "Hold on," I say as I try to get them all on paper.

It's quiet for a second while I try to draft a potential thesis statement.

"Can I ask you a question?"

Something about the tone of his voice makes me stop writing and look up. Usually Isaiah is loud and pushy, but his voice is quiet and slow, and this feels more personal.

"Do you ever see her? Or hear her? Or anything?"

He doesn't have to say who for me to know he means my mom. I don't respond at first. I just stare at him.

"Like, do you think she's a ghost?"

With anyone else, I would probably grunt or run out of the room or something, but the curiosity in his eyes doesn't scare me. It's kind of nice actually. He really seems to want to know. "No. But I keep looking for her."

He sighs. "Yeah, I would, too."

It's possible Isaiah just went from the geeky kid I have to sit next to in science class to my favorite person in the whole world.

Chapter Three

Science class opens a floodgate. I've been trying to pretend that my interest in ghosts hasn't picked up since my mom died, but ever since the accident I've been looking for signs like crazy. At night I beg the stars for just one little moment. A flickering light, a lost pencil showing up unexpectedly, or even that tropical smell I love.

But there's been nothing.

The more Isaiah and I talk, the more I wonder. What does that mean? Is she safely on the other side? Is there another side? If I keep trying, will they let her visit? Just for a second?

The more I think about it, the heavier my head feels. I drag my feet on my way to group therapy. Okay, so they don't call it that. The official name for my next hour of fun is Transitions, which basically means it's whatever elective you signed up for: cooking, just-say-no-to-drugs class, or in my case, group psycho sessions. "Stress management." I was transferred out of computer class a few weeks into the semester, just when we were getting to the fine art of adding animations to PowerPoint slides. Mrs. Carter, the school psychologist I've been visiting a couple of times a week since last spring, thought I needed another outlet for my emotions.

My sister is usually the crabby one. She's the one who can't find the silver lining of a black cloud even if it's glowing. But even I can't stand group therapy.

I pause outside the door. One thing's for sure: it's always an hour of surprises. You never know who's going to be there or what state they'll be in. People skip Transitions classes a lot. Four of us never miss this class, though. Me, obviously. Because even though I hate it here, even though I hate coming, if I don't show up, Mrs. Carter might call my dad. I haven't told him about any of this.

Dylan Fry's always here, too; he's the biggest bully in the school. You'd never know how mean he is from his bright blue eyes, wide smile, and curly brown hair that sticks up all over, but you can hear the grudge in his voice. And no, even though I keep watching for it, I don't think there's a nice guy underneath all that give-me-your-lunch-money attitude. He's pretty much the same in therapy as he is the rest of the time at school. Except he's always there, which sort of makes me think maybe he likes talking about his problems. Or maybe he doesn't want Mrs. Carter to call his home either. I think his grudge is for a good reason; he's never said it out loud, but I get the impression his dad likes to use him for a punching bag.

Next is Amanda Waxler. She's a large girl who wears the same green headband in her straight blond hair every day. She has anger management issues. She breaks things, rarely people.

And finally there's Brian Reed. He's the super-skinny geeky type. He's in all of the smart-kid classes. Brian's dad died about six months before my mom. You'd think that would bond us in some way. In fact, that's exactly what I thought at first. When I first joined Transitions, I couldn't wait to hear what he had to say. I thought we were kind of the same, and I had this idea of us becoming friends,

But then, the second day, I told my story. Most of the kids had probably already heard it. I had been out of school for a while, and I know the teachers knew what had happened. I figured they'd probably warned most of the other kids, so everyone would be "understanding." The early days back then were mostly a fog, but I remember it was the one time I cried in school. When I was finished, everyone got quiet; even Dylan didn't make a single stupid comment. But Brian's eyes pierced me. My eyebrows crinkled in confusion, and I stared back.

Mrs. Carter noticed. "Brian? Do you have something to say?"

"At least she didn't suffer."

His tone smacked me. It wasn't what he said. I'd heard that before. It's one of five million and one things people say that they think will make you feel better. It was how he said it. No one had ever sounded jealous when they said it. *At least she didn't suffer.* He was absolutely green with envy.

It sucked that his dad died. I knew that. Brian's dad was a gym teacher at our school, and he'd been Teacher of the Year for three years in a row. We all knew him and we all liked him, too. He got cancer. A bad one. He was gone in six months.

But I was furious. "At least you got to say good-bye."

"It isn't a contest, Andie." Mrs. Carter looked back and forth between us. I wished I was the one with the anger problem.

And I've learned that she's flat-out wrong on that one. Group therapy *is* a contest. We work hard to outdo each other in the my-life-sucks game.

Other than the regulars, lots of kids come and go. They have all kinds of problems. There's a girl who thinks she's too fat, a boy whose locker contents got him dragged out by the police, and another girl who doesn't talk much but just seems sad all the time.

I still hate Brian Reed. I hate him because we are never going to be friends even though we have something so important in common. But every time he starts talking, it's so obvious he really believes he has it the worst.

"You can't understand what it's like," he said once. "My dad was my best friend. I don't even have anyone to help with my homework anymore." My fists clenched at my sides. I have to take a deep breath not to explode when he says stuff like that. We mostly ignore him. But every once in a while one of us can't stand it anymore. A couple of weeks ago, Dylan rolled his eyes and cut in. "Give me a break, dork. Your problem is you had it too good before. And now you don't know how to handle a little bad crap. You know what, you've still got more good every day than I've had my whole life."

Okay, so maybe sometimes I get a clue that there's something more there with Dylan. But I still try not to make eye contact with him, because he can be scary. I don't have any money for him to steal, but he's not picky—he collects notebooks, pencils, iPods.

That day when Dylan blew up, everyone went quiet, waiting to see what Brian would do.

He cried. Hard.

And Mrs. Carter yelled at Dylan. I'm not sure that was fair. I think Dylan has a point. Because I know about Before and After, too. My family wasn't perfect Before, and life still had bumps, but they weren't a big deal. A bad grade on a test. A girl who makes fun of your hair for being too curly or your nose for being too wide. Parents who argue over stupid stuff like bills or dishes left in the sink. I remember getting really upset about stuff like that. My dad used to laugh at me and pop me on the nose. "Yeah, you have such a stressful life, Andie. Maybe you should retire early."

I would roll my eyes at him, cross my arms, and grumble under my breath. He just didn't understand. So I kind of get where Brian is coming from, too. He really believes no one understands. That things *are* that bad. But he's the one who really doesn't get it.

When Mrs. Carter calls the group to order today, it's clear from the beginning that Brian is in rare form. "I mean, how can she just go on a date? Doesn't she love him anymore?"

Mrs. Carter nods and scans the other group members expectantly. But Brian just keeps going.

"I don't think my dad would have wanted her to move on like that. She's really selfish. And my grandma keeps telling her it's a great idea to get out there again. Why? To prove my dad didn't matter?"

Inside, I'm like a simmering pot of water. Lots of bubbles hanging out at the bottom of the pot. Almost there.

"Sometimes I wish it had been my mom instead of my dad who got sick."

And suddenly I'm at a full boil, popping and raging. "Shut up! Just shut up!"

Everyone turns to stare at me. Mrs. Carter's mouth is wide open. Before she can say anything, I let myself boil over.

"Do you hear yourself? Do you hear the people in here? Would you just stop whining? Your dad died. It sucks. I get it. Believe me, *I get it*. But you're not the only one with problems. Not by a long shot. And maybe you're not ready for your mom to move on, but you should be happy she's at least in the land of the living. I bet she still buys groceries and hasn't wasted your family's money. I bet she still tells you she loves you and hugs you and says everything is going to be okay!" With that I run out of breath.

And then I sit back and wait for Mrs. Carter to send me out of the room. I fold my arms and stare at my lap. I glance up only once to see Amanda smiling, and then I hear Dylan clap.

Of course, Brian bursts into tears.

When I look up again, Mrs. Carter's expression is pure panic. Paige tells me that I shouldn't trust the school psychologist. She says they think they can change the world, but they aren't prepared to handle real problems. I can practically see Mrs. Carter's heart racing in her eyes. She glances toward the clock and smiles weakly.

"Well, uh, it seems time is almost up."

We all turn our heads toward the clock to check. There's still five minutes until the bell will actually ring, but maybe we're all relieved to let this drop.

Mrs. Carter spends a few minutes reminding us all of the rules of our support group and encouraging us to start planning for the summer. "Some of you may find that when you don't have this regular discussion time, you'll get overwhelmed."

Dylan rolls his eyes, and Amanda snorts. I think Mrs. Carter might cry, but she doesn't.

I don't want to talk to her *at all*, so I have my bag ready to go so I can race out the door when the bell finally rings. I'm so sure she's going to try to stop me that I go the long way around the room to avoid her. I wonder if she really is as freaked out by my outburst as I am, because I don't hear her call my name.

When I turn around on my way out the door—just because I'm curious—I find that she's patting Brian on the shoulder.

I glare in her direction and shake my head. I don't want her to chase after me, but the fact that she's more interested in whiny Brian than what I just admitted makes me mad. Or it hurts. Or maybe both. I'm even more surprised when I get halfway down the hall and I feel Dylan punch me lightly on the arm. "Hey, kid. Sorry."

I nod. "Thanks." But he's already pushing some sixth grader into a locker and laughing.

Chapter Four

The best thing I can say about the afternoon is that it ends. I walk home these days because Paige's shift at the diner starts right after school. We live almost a mile from school, which is just perfect, because if it were a mile or more, I'd get to ride the bus. But no, we are like .99999 miles away. It's drizzling when I leave today, so I pull the hood of my sweatshirt around my ears, point my face down, and take off.

A block from school, a horn blasts, and I look up.

"You need a ride?" Isaiah grins as he leans out a car window.

The woman in the driver's seat waves me toward the car, so I hop in the back.

"This must be the infamous science partner you can't stop talking about."

Isaiah looks at the woman with wide eyes and his mouth falls open. "Mooommm."

I'm sure I blush.

"Where to?"

I give her directions and I'm sure to thank her several times. Then we drive in silence.

Isaiah turns around as far as his seat belt will let him. "Why are you so quiet?"

"I'm not."

"Yes, you are. You were all excited during class. Now it's like someone kicked you in the gut."

"Not the best afternoon, I guess."

"Isaiah, maybe she doesn't want to discuss it with you." His mom looks at me through the rearview mirror and smiles.

"I'm going to start researching tonight," he says, practically bouncing. I've never known anyone so excited about a school project. I give him a halfhearted smile.

"Cool."

He keeps talking, and his mom shakes her head. At one point she puts her hand on his knee and gives him one of those warning looks. Sometimes, it's the little things. Like that look. I can't swallow, and I close my eyes. This day needs to end. I have good days, too. This just hasn't been one of them. Not by a long shot.

When she pulls in front of my house, Isaiah's mom scans the windows. "Is anyone home?"

"I'm not sure," I say.

"Do you need to call anyone?" she asks.

"No, it's all good. Thanks so much."

As I shut the door, she rolls her window down. "Andie?"

"Yeah?"

"Are you sure you're okay?"

I take a deep breath and nod. "I'll be fine. It was just a bad day. Really."

That seems to reassure her. "Feel free to call if you need anything."

Oh, I know this script. "Thanks, I will." *Hi, do you think you could pay my dad's electric bill? Or maybe put gas in my sister's car? That's not what you meant? Oh, I'm sorry. Well, thanks for the offer.*

I punch in the code on the garage door keypad. When the door starts to rise, I see the wheels of my dad's truck. My heart rate picks up, and I pull my backpack tighter. I'm not used to seeing much of him at all anymore, but definitely not after school and not when Paige isn't here. She does most of the talking/accusing/yelling. I walk slowly through the garage, and a thought hits me. What if something's wrong?

Right after the accident, I woke up every night and snuck into his room. I stood next to him until he rolled over or snored. Anything to let me know he was alive. I couldn't lose both of them. For weeks, I followed him around like a new puppy. If he went to the grocery store, I tagged along. I even joined him at the gym. I would hop on a bike even though I was bored to tears, just so I didn't let him out of my sight. After a while though, the excuses came. "Sorry, Andie, but I'm just going to hit the gym on the way home from work to save time," or "I've got to work late, so I'm skipping my workout tonight."

He may not be the dad that used to make me laugh every day, but I know I want him to be okay when I walk through the door.

I pause inside the garage, but, finally, I take the plunge and step into the house. I drop my backpack on the floor and shut the door behind me. I hesitate, listening for sound. I take a few more steps and suddenly my nose is blasted with the best smell in the whole world.

Spaghetti.

I'm absolutely not kidding. Yeah, sure, I like chocolate chip cookies and brownies as much as everybody else, but the sound of boiling noodles and the smell of simmering sauce always makes everything better. Even on a day like today.

It pulls me forward, and I run into the kitchen. My dad stands in front of the stove, stirring with a big green spoon.

He smiles when he sees me. My skin tingles with hope, and I rock on my toes. I want to rush over and fall into his arms, but something stops me. It's like this is a mirage. I can't trust it.

"Hey, Andie."

"Hi. What's up?" I still don't move.

"Not much. I noticed we were low on food today, so I made a grocery run."

"Did you tell Paige? She's going to be so relieved that . . ." I trail off when I realize I'm about to say that she'll be able to give me some lunch money.

His face falls and he rubs his right temple. I'm afraid I'll lose him before I get him back.

"No big deal. I'll text her, okay?" He shrugs.

"It's early," I say.

"Huh?"

"For spaghetti." I move toward the cabinet that holds the strainers, pull one out, and place it in the sink before he responds.

"Oh, well, I can't stay long. I just thought you might be hungry."

Something in his tone feels weird. The whole thing feels weird. I turn around, my eyes narrowed. "What's going on?"

Instead of answering, he motions with his head for me to move as he walks over with the pot of noodles. I stare while he dumps the contents into the sink, steam rising instantly.

I grab a couple of bowls and hold one out to him.

He considers it for a second. "I'm not really hungry."

The disappointment must show on my face. I bet my shoulders slump or something, because he quickly changes his mind. "Maybe just a little."

I heap my bowl to the top.

"You won't have room for meatballs," he says.

"Meatballs? You made meatballs?" It's Christmas and a birthday party rolled into one. Maybe even a new puppy and summer vacation.

"You bet. I even splurged on the non-generic brand."

I giggle. It's an ongoing joke in our house. Or it used to be. Mom always bought generic, unless Dad went shopping with her.

I burn my tongue on my first bite, and I've stuffed my mouth so full of meatball that all I can do is open wide and fan it with my hand to cool it down.

My dad laughs and pours me a glass of milk. He bought milk, too.

"You really must be hungry," he says, but as soon as it's out his mouth, he stops laughing, and his eyes don't smile anymore.

"Really, what's going on?" I ask again.

He runs a hand through his dark brown hair. It's longer now than it used to be. Mom always teased him and called him Paul McCartney when it got too long. Even though his bangs flop down a bit, I can see the past year in the lines at the corners of his deeply set eyes and the crinkles in his forehead. I don't remember them being there before. He rests his elbow on the table and leans into it. "I got a call from a woman at the school. Apparently, there were some signs today that you didn't have enough food."

I've just taken a huge bite. I'd wrapped like six pieces of spaghetti all around my fork and shoved the whole thing in at once, so I can't answer him.

"You know, I wish you wouldn't talk to the school about stuff like this. You could just talk to me, you know."

My throat tightens and the food is stuck. I really wish Paige were here. I know she'd say something mean but honest, like, *Sure, I'll try that next time you're passed out.* I'd hate that she said it, but I wish I wasn't scared to be as honest.

"I didn't." And it's not a lie. I didn't really talk about the money and food stuff with anyone. Not on purpose anyway.

"She said you meet with her sometimes."

I swallow my mouthful of spaghetti, and I fear that the next bite won't taste as good. I don't like where this is headed.

"Yeah."

"What do you talk about?"

Don't blow this, I tell myself. I hear how hard he's trying to control his voice. I don't know what's behind this, but I sense fear. Maybe anger, too.

"Just, stuff, you know?"

"No, I don't know. What do you tell her?"

"Nothing really. She just asks about how I'm feeling."

"What do you say?"

"It depends, I guess. Today wasn't a good day."

He sighs. And for a second his face melts. I watch the fear, the anger, the grief fall off layer by layer. He reaches out and grabs my hand. "I have a lot of those."

"I know," I whisper.

As fast as he thawed, he freezes again. "Do you talk about me with that woman?"

My dad squeezes my hand while he says it. He might think he's reassuring me, but it just feels like pressure. Crushing pressure.

"No." *Yes.*

"That's . . . good. Not that you shouldn't talk about how you feel. It's just that I know things haven't been the best around here. People don't always understand what it's like for us, do they?"

I shake my head.

"Right, so it could get complicated if you talk about things like, you know, today and the groceries."

"But I didn't—" I start to protest. But he pats my arm.

"Let's just keep our problems to ourselves, okay?"

My leg shakes under the table. Paige's voice echoes in my ears. *Yes, I can see how that's working out so well for you.* My own voice stays silent as I nod my head.

"You're always such a good girl. So, listen, the fridge is stocked for a while, and there's a new video game out there for you." This is weird, because I don't really play video games. He stands and starts to leave.

"Where are you going?"

"I, uh, I have to go. Out. I shouldn't be too late."

Liar. "You could stay. Maybe we could play the game together?"

He pretends to think about it for a second. "Soon. Okay?"

"Sure." *Never.*

And he's gone with a wave. I hear the garage door open and the car start. I let my fork fall.

I leave my spaghetti sitting in the bowl. I can't eat it right now. I'm mad. And I'm sad. It's not fair, and it feels like I've jumped straight into a freezing pool of water. It's so cold it burns. I will never get used to this. Will anything ever feel good again? Maybe I should just give up on him. It's almost too hard to deal with the disappointment when what you hope for never comes true.

I push my chair in. Super loud. I throw the stupid video game across the room. I yell at the top of my lungs and, when that doesn't help, I punch the pillows on the couch. I slam shut the door to the laundry room, just because I happen to see it open. Finally, I'm beat. I've wasted every emotion on this awful day. I'm not sure what hurts more—that my dad was more worried about himself than finding out that I hadn't had anything to eat today, or that he's in there. I saw it. I felt it when he touched my hand. My dad is in there somewhere, and I didn't know just how badly I wanted him back. All that time I worried about losing him too, and he was already gone.

I collapse down on the couch, and I'm out.

Chapter Five

When I wake up, I jump, afraid I'm late for school. It takes a minute before I put together what happened. I glance at the clock on the DVD player. It's six o'clock, so I've been out almost two hours. I feel groggy from my nap. I head to the kitchen and groan when I see the spaghetti mess. I put the leftovers in plastic containers, popping one meatball in my mouth as I clean the pots.

I need to call my sister, but I'm on edge. I don't want to be alone in this house right now. Isaiah's question about ghosts echoes in my head. The only ghosts here seem to be Paige and Dad.

I decide to visit Paige at the diner. It takes me about a half hour on foot, but I can use the fresh air, and it's still light in the spring evenings. When she first started working there, my mom and I would stop in a lot on the weekends. Paige used to get so mad. "Why are you embarrassing me?" she'd ask my mom.

"I'm just trying to give you good tips. Apple pie à la mode, please."

I have a usual. Hot fudge sundae with whipped cream, three cherries, and no nuts.

When she sees me walk in, Paige waves me to a seat and heads immediately to the ice cream freezer. If it's a slow night, and her manager isn't paying attention, I eat for free. Otherwise, she drops money from her tips into the register.

"Sorry about this morning again," she says when she puts the sundae in front of me.

"Dad bought groceries," I say before popping the cherry in my mouth.

"Really?"

"Yeah. I guess the school counselor called him."

"Oh."

"He made me spaghetti."

She raises an eyebrow. I watch the flicker of hope in her eyes. "Where is he now?"

"Out."

"Oh," she says again.

"He doesn't want me to see Mrs. Carter."

"How did that come up?"

"I guess someone called him today. I fell asleep in class, and then I kind of went off on some kid in group. And I might have mentioned not eating much."

Her eyes widen. "Ah."

"What's wrong?"

"Well, you know, sometimes if they think a parent can't take care of their kid, they take them away."

"Take them away?"

"Sure, they find a different home for them."

I've just taken a bite of whipped cream and I spit it out. "I didn't know. Should I stop going to see her?"

Paige takes a breath and then glances around the diner. "Do you like going?"

"I don't know. Yes. No. It depends. I don't like group."

She laughs and turns around, grabs a pot of coffee, and does a quick loop around to the four or so customers in the place. Paige looks a lot like my mom—same nose for sure—and they're the most alike, too. Both of them are stubborn and like to be in control. Paige can be emotional like Dad sometimes, but she's mostly just like Mom. You'd think people who were so much alike would get along perfectly, but Dad says that's why they fought so much. I've always been somewhere in the middle, I guess.

When she gets back, she leans on the counter and gets her face close to mine. "You got it the worst, Andie Candy, so if you want to go talk to the shrink dink, you do it, okay?"

She leans over and kisses me on the cheek.

"Mrs. Carter says it isn't a contest."

"Well, it's sure not one you want to win, but you know, I've only got a few months before I can move out or go to college or something. And you've got to go through a lot of crap in the next few years without Mom."

"You, too."

"Yeah."

"And, I guess, so does Dad."

Paige's mouth falls open a second. Then she swallows. "You're too smart, you know that?"

"Tell that to my math teacher."

And just like that, we're laughing, and she's telling me horror stories of the worst teachers she's ever had. She wrinkles her nose when she talks about the one who used to clip his toenails during class. That's something Mom always did when something grossed her out, too.

For the second time today, I get a glimpse. I know that things can be different. Better. Never the same, but better than they are right now.

I just don't know how to get us there.

I hang out the rest of the night with Paige. I try to figure out what might get my dad to try harder and what would make Paige smile more. I doodle on a place mat. I list things they like: movies, friends, cookies, concerts. But those are all temporary fixes. I could try to get them to go do something, but even if that made things better, it wouldn't last. It would just be for a couple of hours. I want more normal. Closer to normal, anyway.

I start drawing a face, and when I'm done, I realize I've sketched my mom. I look down at her. She was the glue, and without her, maybe we'll never stick together again.

But I don't want to believe it. There must be a way to make things better.

By the time I walk into science class the next day, I'm thoroughly discouraged again. I've considered things every which way, and no matter how I see it, only Mom can save us, and she's gone. Isaiah plops down next to me, waving a bunch of papers.

"Research!" he says. He's bouncing up and down as usual, and his grin takes over his whole face.

I can't help laughing.

"There's so much cool stuff about ghosts."

I roll my eyes. "I bet you found a lot of funny stuff on the Internet."

"You would not believe the crazy. But I don't even mean that. I mean the science. It's awesome. People have analyzed the chemical makeup of antimatter and air quality and even sonic stuff. The theories are endless. So we've got to narrow in for sure. We can talk about whether or not ghosts are real, but there's probably still too much information on that. I like physics the best, so I'd like to go that route."

"Physics?"

"Sure, like motion and stuff? How ghosts move, how we sense their movement. Trajectories—stuff like that."

"There's real research on this?"

"Uh-huh. Tons. A lot of people are really into paranormal activity."

"Huh." I guess I never thought about it much before. I like ghost stories, but I hadn't really considered the work people might do to prove ghosts exist. Other than the crazy *Ghostbusters* types.

"Why are you surprised? I don't get it. Like you said yesterday, don't you think a lot of people want ghosts to exist?"

And it's like fireworks explode in my head. I throw my hands up. "That's it!"

"What?"

I stare at Isaiah for a second, not sure whether I should tell him. But in the end, he's the only person I *can* tell.

"Why do you think that most people want ghosts to be real?"

He puts the tip of his pencil against his cheek. "Because they miss someone."

"Right. And why do they do things like Ouija boards and séances?"

"So they can talk to the person they love."

"Uh-huh. They're hoping for a message. A chance to know how things are . . . on the other side."

"Okaaay." He drags out the word, not following what any of this has to do with the project. It doesn't.

"I think there's something else, too. It's not just that they want their loved ones to be okay. *They* want to be okay. They want to know that their loved ones still miss them. Still know about them."

"Is that—is that what you feel?"

I shrug.

"Is this something you want to study?"

I shake my head. "No, this is something else. Something big. But it's just between you and me, you understand? You can't tell anyone."

We must be getting too loud, because our teacher comes over and stands beside us.

"How's the project going?"

I have a moment of panic where I think we're going to get in trouble, but Isaiah flips his notebook open and holds up a very detailed outline of ideas and research questions.

"Great!" he says with a big fake smile. "We're studying ghosts."

Mr. Sneed's eyes narrow and he looks at me. He raises an eyebrow, but then gives the paper a once-over. "This is . . . interesting. I think this could come together pretty well."

Satisfied, he moves over to another table.

"Spill," Isaiah says.

"Wow, you're good."

He waves a hand. He already knows that.

"Isaiah, things at home aren't so good."

"I kind of figured. What's going on?"

"We're falling apart. My dad lost his job. And he goes out a lot. To the casino and bars, places like that." I whisper the last part and wait for him to respond. Thankfully, he doesn't say anything; he just nods very slowly. So I take a deep breath. "I've been trying to think of a way to make everyone normal again, but I think my mom is what kept us all together and right and everything. She managed us."

"Moms are kind of like that, huh?"

I don't want to tell him I think my mom was special. I'm sure he thinks his mom is too, but . . .

"Anyway, I think maybe my mom is the only one who can save us."

His face twists up and he sets his pencil down on the table. "You've lost me."

"It's your idea, and you don't even know it: ghosts."

"Still lost."

"What if my mom came back? What if she haunted my family? Maybe they'd listen to her."

Isaiah's mouth forms an O, and he leans back in his chair. He taps the pencil on his desk for a few seconds. I let him think, hoping it will all come to him like magic, and he'll understand. Suddenly he starts to rifle through his papers. He lays out a blank one and pulls a printed article from the stack in his folder. "Here are some of the common things they say ghosts do. Sounds are the big one. Not just the typical stuff like creaking floorboards and groaning pipes, but music, and even voices. That seems doable, but maybe complicated."

When Isaiah looks up from his writing, now *I* am bouncing in my seat, and I would clap if it wouldn't make me look like a total dork. He turns his head slowly to face me.

"It's been a long time since I've seen you smile."

My brow furrows. "I smile."

"Not like that," he says. "That's the real one, not the one you put on for show."

My face burns and I bite my lip. I motion toward the paper. "What about smells?"

Chapter Six

I can barely contain my excitement for the rest of the day. I realize it's a strange thing to be excited about, but it's just been so long since I had something to look forward to. Something, anything, that might make a difference. And, yeah, it gives me an excuse to think about my mom.

So I smile more all afternoon, and people notice. After school, my friends gather around my locker.

"Hey, are you still on for Friday?" Becki asks.

"Sure," I say, maybe a little too quickly.

She crosses her arms and her face scrunches up. "What's up with you?"

"I don't know. Why?"

"You're too happy today."

Leah interrupts. "I know! It's a *boooy*, right?"

Becki laughs. "No-brainer—it's got to be Isaiah." They all burst into giggles. I'm still in too good a mood to be offended, but I start to protest on his behalf.

Gisela saves me. "So, is it a boy or not?"

"Sheesh, I'm just in a good mood. I can get crabby again if you want."

"No, no, happy is good. Anyway, we talked Leah—Miss Super Serious—into joining us for the sleepover." She nods toward Leah. "So we're all in."

"But you all have to help me study," Leah adds. When Becki rolls her eyes and Gisela laughs, she gets louder. "I mean it. You promised."

Becki waves a hand. "I know, I know. It's fine. I think the plan is for everyone to ride home with me, if that's okay."

I still love the idea of the sleepover. I mean, maybe Becki's been weird lately, but we have *the best* sleepovers, especially at Becki's because her dad doesn't care how late we stay up. One time, we forced ourselves to stay up all night long. If anyone fell asleep, even for a second, we tickled them awake and then they had to do whatever dare we gave them. Leah cleaned the toilet with her socks. I ate a pickle dipped in chocolate. Actually, it wasn't as bad I thought it would be, but I pretended to gag so they didn't make me do something else instead. I'd give anything for that kind of night again, even if I had to run around the block in a swimsuit singing "I'm a Little Teapot" like Gisela did. I miss how easy it all was, how silly we could be, and yeah, going home in the morning to a clean house, a full fridge, and my mom.

Now, though, I have plans to put in motion for my project, and I stop to think about how the sleepover will affect my schedule. Should I get started with my haunting plan tonight? Or should I wait for Saturday when I can fully commit? I can't wait to find out how Paige and my dad will react. Will they even notice? I'm not planning to be too obvious. What am I even planning?

Everyone else takes off to catch their buses, and I take my time walking down the eighth grade hall. It smells rank—like sticking your head inside of a sock someone wore for a week, or taking a whiff of garbage that's been sitting outside in the summer. Isaiah didn't think smells were as important as some of the other senses based on the paranormal research, but I've decided it's the best way for me to start. I have a list of the five scents I most associate with my mom. First, there's the tropical spray for sure; then sunscreen—they're similar but different—the spray is more breezy, the sunscreen more heavy; and oranges. She had an orange-scented air freshener in her car, so every time you got in it felt fresh and summery, and it made me crave breakfast food even when she picked me up after school.

I thought about adding spaghetti to my list, but it's more of family food than really one of my mom's scents. No, my mom's food smell is *bacon*. I had to stop myself from laughing out loud when it hit me while I was trying correct my tennis serve in PE. My mom made bacon at least once a week, and the smell lingered for hours and hours after. It seeped into her hair, so we'd be at a softball game or the mall and she'd get frustrated. "Most women smell like a lush garden, and I'm pig meat."

My dad would tease her. "And if more women knew just how hot that was, they'd be bottling up eau de bacon by the gallons and charging a thousand dollars an ounce for it."

"Excellent. That can be my claim to fame. I'll invent a whole line of comfort-food cologne and market it to women. They say the way to a man's heart is through his stomach. Well, skip the cooking."

So, definitely bacon.

And finally, her hair spray. If Dad was around when she got ready, he made her spray in the living room so the bathroom didn't become a cloud of chemicals. She bought these super-sized silver bottles at the expensive natural-products store, but they sure didn't smell natural.

I know that I can't use too many at once, and some smells are going to be tricky. Like bacon. If it's too strong, they'll know that someone just cooked it, and that's not what I'm going for. Plus, I'd have to hide the bacon or eat a whole pound and the grease, and that just seems way too difficult for a Thursday afternoon. Especially if either my dad or Paige happens to be home.

I know we don't have any of Mom's hair spray in the house because Dad cleaned out their bathroom a few months ago. No way can I get to that special store, and I don't have thirty dollars for a can anyway. So my options are sunscreen, body spray, or oranges. Tough call. Anything in spray form is definitely the easiest, and as luck would have it, I grabbed the travel bottle of my mom's tropical body spray that my dad had tossed into the garbage pile when he cleaned out all Mom's stuff. I couldn't rescue everything, but I tucked that in my pocket and ran to my room. I've had the precious contraband hidden in my bottom drawer all this time. It's perfect.

But where to spray?

I've completed a full logistical analysis (Isaiah's words, not mine) of all possible spray locations by the time I get home. I've identified two perfect spots. The only way the plan works is if my dad's not home, and I'm relieved when I open the garage door and his car is gone.

I race up the stairs and grab the bottle. Though it's small, it's still pretty full. It'll do the job just fine. Even though no one is home, I'm nervous about going into my parents' room, so I open my dad's door slowly.

There's a part of me that forgets his car is gone and worries my dad might be home in the middle of the day again, but I think I might also still wonder if it's possible that my mom's ghost *has* been hiding in here all this time. Maybe he's keeping her to himself. As weird as it sounds, I giggle at the idea.

I'm surprised to find how dark the room is. I don't remember it being like this. The curtains are shut tight, and all the lights are off. The bed is unmade. More than that, it's like it was never made in the first place. The covers are bunched at the bottom, and the fitted sheet has come off the end so the mattress is exposed. Around the bed, clothes are scattered everywhere, and I can barely see the floor.

I thought I might feel closer to her when I walked into the room, but the thing that hits me is the absence of her. If I didn't know what this room had been before, I wouldn't have any idea that she'd ever lived here. All that time I spent standing outside the door hoping to catch a bit of her smell was a waste of time. I can't see her. I can't smell her. The smell is closer to the tang of the eighth grade hallway than what I'd expect from my parents' room. I don't know how long I stand by the doorway, taking it all in. I know I should just do what I planned to do and get out, but I can't. There's too much I want to know.

I move slowly, practically hugging the wall, afraid to fall in. The grief in this room feels like a black hole. I get to the dresser and run a finger across the top. I let loose a layer of dust, and it makes me cough. I open the top drawer, but shut it again when all I see is a bunch of my dad's underwear.

The next drawer holds T-shirts and socks. I gently push the socks around. I start to pick up the shirts, and that's when I see a small black box tucked in beneath them. My fingers tremble as I pick it up and open the lid. My heart leaps into my mouth. A thick gold wedding ring—my dad's—gleams, even in the dark room. And, to my surprise, it's partnered with my mom's rings. I have to sit down, and I slide to the floor. She had two rings. The first has a simple solitaire diamond, soldered to a thin gold band. The second is the diamond band my dad gave her for their tenth wedding anniversary. She cried when she opened the velvet box. But she was afraid to wear it, so it stayed in her jewelry box most of the time. I glance up at her dresser, but it's not sitting on top anymore. What happened to her jewelry box?

I pick up her original ring and slide it onto one of my fingers. It's obviously way too big, but I hold it in place and wriggle my finger to watch the diamond sparkle. I thought her rings were all gone. I remembered seeing them both on her finger at the wake. How did they get here? I turn them with my fingers, watching the diamonds sparkle. Here she is. Tingles run down my arms.

If I feel like this just holding her rings, maybe there's hope for my plan. I put the rings back in the box and tuck it into its spot under the shirts. I wipe away a couple of tears and then I focus on my mission.

I head over to the bed and pull the little bottle out of my pocket. The pillows are stacked, and I slide the bottom one out and place it on what was my mom's side of the bed. Then I squirt the bottle, once. I can't help but let the beachy smell wash over me. When I open my eyes, I immediately notice the time on the alarm clock on the night stand, and I pick up my pace. After making sure everything is back in its place and looks untouched, I run down the stairs and into the family room. I walk right up to the couch, and I press the pump just above the cushion on her side of the couch.

I race back up the stairs to my room. I am careful to hide the body spray in the back of my closet, inside my old box of Barbies. Then I take my clothes off, leave them in my laundry basket, and hop in the shower. I am careful to scrub hard and use plenty of Dial soap, and then I let the water wash away every last bit of my mom's scent.

After the shower, I throw on a pair of shorts and a T-shirt, and I gather the laundry from Paige's room and combine it with mine. I toss it all into the machine with some soap and press START. I don't want anyone to be able to connect me to the smell.

For good measure, I decide to make dinner. I resist the urge to go with BLTs. That would be too much. Instead, I throw a frozen pizza in the oven. That should do the trick. The body spray smell won't hit until one of them sits down on the couch or my dad lies down in bed.

I pace, waiting for them to come home. I want to see their reactions. Will they say anything to me? I doubt Dad would, but Paige might.

She arrives home about fifteen minutes later.

"Mmm, you made dinner?" she calls out.

I answer from the dining room where I sit with my laptop, looking up some of the links Isaiah gave me today. "Just a frozen pizza."

"Smells good," she says, and I smile.

I stand up to get us plates. Paige has already cut the pizza into several large pieces. "I'm starving," she says.

I hand her an empty plate.

"Thanks. Wanna pop in a movie?"

"Sure. Don't you have homework?"

"Yeah, but I want to sit for a while. I've been doing a lot of shifts lately. I'm just happy to have the evening off. They tried to call me in, but I said no. I could barely stay awake during history today."

"That happens to me every day," I say. "And I don't have a job."

She tousles my hair and stuffs her mouth with pizza. "Last one in's a rotten egg."

I don't bother trying to race her. I've never been the fastest. Besides, I'm hoping she'll pick Mom's old spot. My face falls when I see her sitting on the opposite side of the couch. She's already picked up the remote. I plop down on the easy chair. It's usually my dad's spot, but I want to give her room on the couch so maybe she'll still smell the spray. I chew and watch the movie as it starts. Honestly, I'm having a hard time paying attention. I keep looking over at my sister to see if she's noticed anything, but she stares blankly at the screen. I figure she's probably too far away, and I wonder how long the body spray's fragrance will be noticeable.

"Oh, I'm going to a sleepover at Becki's tomorrow night."

"Did you ask Dad?"

I raise an eyebrow.

She shrugs. "Well, leave a note. How are you getting there?"

"Riding home after school."

"Sounds good. I won't be here anyway."

She yawns and leans back into the couch. *Please lie down,* I say in my head, willing her to sink closer to the magic spot.

"Any other plans for the weekend?" I ask.

She shakes her head and yawns again. "Work and sleep."

She slides down a little more.

"No parties or anything?"

She snorts. "No, no parties."

She yawns one more time, and it takes over her whole face. That did it. She lets her head fall down to the other end of the couch and puts her feet up. It doesn't happen instantly. In fact, I think she might fall asleep without noticing anything, but a few seconds later, I see her eyes fly open, and she grips the side of the couch. I hear a small intake of breath.

"What's up?"

Her eyes narrow. "Nothing."

I turn back to the TV, but I angle myself so that I can still watch every move she makes, at least from the side. I can tell she's trying to be sneaky. She turns over like she's going to fall asleep, and I notice her take a deep breath. I wish I could see her face.

She twists back around, and I blink, trying to make sure my eyes are still focused on the television. *Come on, Paige. Tell me what you're thinking. Or, at least, show me.*

She does. It's just not exactly what I was hoping for. Paige stands. "I'm going to my room."

It's practically a whisper, and her voice shakes as she says it.

"Okay," I say. "You all right?"

She nods, but doesn't say anything else. Later, she comes back downstairs to get her backpack. Her eyes are red and puffy. I want to tell her I'm sorry. And I even think I've made a huge mistake. Maybe I won't do it again.

But I've got to. I've got to see it through to know for sure. After all, things can't get worse. Besides, I think it's like Mom used to say about dinner: "No dessert if you don't eat something green." Paige used to claim that green Jell-O should count. My mom would laugh and list all kinds of things where you had to have something bad happen before the good could come. "Spring follows winter. Birth follows labor—"

"Okay, okay, I'll eat the stupid broccoli."

It might hurt, but I'm hoping there will be dessert at the end of this.

Chapter Seven

My alarm clock is a hammer that hits me over the head again and again. I swat at it and fall back asleep, twice. I stayed up way too late last night reading ghost stories and thinking up new experiments. I didn't want Paige or my dad to see light under the door and come in to find me with my charts and ghost research, so I turned off the lights and hid under my covers, using a flashlight to see my notes. I must have dozed off, because the flashlight is still on next to me, and I'm tucked under my bedspread. It's still dark out, but I throw the covers off and stand, stretching. I shake the fog away and go over my plan in my head. Since I'm going to the sleepover right after school, if I want to get another haunting under way, it has to be before I wake up Paige.

I came up with this plan last night, and it's genius, if I say so myself. Paige uses an old cloth messenger bag for school every day. I pop downstairs and go straight to our family's Great Eyesore, as my mom used to call it. We don't have a real mudroom. Just a bunch of hooks on the wall as you come in from the garage. Jackets, umbrellas, and book bags all hang crookedly, while shoes are piled up on the floor below. Paige's bag didn't even make it onto a hook last night; she must have tossed it on the floor when she got home. Most of the bag is red and white striped canvas, but the strap is just white—grayed from use, but white. I grab the bottle of sunscreen and apply just a little to my hands, then rub it into the bottom of the strap. Just enough so she'll notice the smell most of the day, but it might be hard for her to figure out why. I wash my hands and run back upstairs to get her moving.

I'm surprised to find my dad's door isn't shut. It's wide open. And when I stick my head inside, I discover that he's not there.

I listen for a second in case he's in the bathroom, but there are no sounds. He must have come home at some point, but then where did he go? I don't get an answer until after I'm showered and dressed. I'm dousing a bowl of Rice Krispies—or rather, the generic Crispy Rice—with milk, when I notice noise coming from the family room. I set my bowl down and walk over to the door. The TV is on, and my dad is sprawled out on the couch.

He must hear me come in because he says, "Mornin'."

"How long have you been up?" I ask.

"Pretty much all night."

That explains the empty bedroom. "Couldn't sleep?"

"Not in the least."

"Do you need anything?" I ask. "Are you sick?"

"Nah, just bad dreams, you know?" He turns away from me and rubs his face.

"I do," I say softly.

I leave him and head back to my cereal. By now, Paige has made her way to the kitchen and is filling up a bowl of her own. "Eat it while we got it, right?"

I nod and chew.

"So he's out there?"

I nod again. And chew some more.

"Must be something in the water." She pauses, puts the box of cereal back in the cabinet, then adds, "Or the air."

I gulp my Crispy Rice. "Huh?"

She sits down at the table next to me and speaks quietly. "Last night, it was so weird. I could swear I smelled Mom's perfume. You know that tropical island breeze crap she bought in bulk?"

I bite my lip and smile. "I loved that stuff."

"Really? I couldn't stand it. Made me gag." She takes a bite and swallows quickly. "Anyway, I just missed her more last night."

"I'm sorry."

"Not your fault."

But it is, and I can't tell her. I realize that I have to work faster or differently or something. Because one random encounter is kind of sad. There has to be a message behind it. It's not really a haunting if you don't know a ghost is there. The sunscreen should help to build on what I started last night. But maybe Paige needs a little more help to understand it.

"Sometimes, I hope to catch that smell. You know, like, just a thought that she's around a little, somewhere. Not really here, but here."

A corner of her mouth curves up.

"I hadn't thought about it like that."

"So, maybe—maybe you're kind of lucky. Maybe she just wanted you to know she's around or something."

"Oh my gosh, don't go bringing in your stupid novels. You know what I think about all those ghost stories."

She winks, and then we both rush to finish our cereal. I might have pushed it, but I'm also glad she dropped it when she did. She isn't suspicious. It was just the itty-bittiest hint.

We both head to our rooms to get ready and gather our stuff for school. I notice my palms feel greasy when I head back downstairs. After our breakfast talk, I wonder how she will react to the book bag. I watch from the door as Paige puts on her shoes in the entryway. She picks up the scent before she even makes it to her book bag—I see her stop and sniff the air, almost like a dog. Then she crinkles her nose and throws the bag over her shoulder.

It occurs to me then that it's possible Paige doesn't link Mom to sunscreen the way I do. After all, she didn't love the body spray; she might not even associate the same smells with Mom at all. Shoot. That might change things.

She turns to face me. "Do you eat lunch outside?"

"Sometimes."

She reaches to the shelf above where we hang the bags and grabs the sunscreen bottle. "Here, put this on in the car. Better buttered than burned."

I'm sure my eyes go wide, and I have to suck in my cheeks to prevent the huge smile that's creeping out. That's exactly what Mom used to say when we'd complain about how nasty the stuff made us feel. One time, after Mom had made us slather ourselves in sunscreen, Paige said she felt like someone had taken a stick of butter and melted it on top of her. The phrase stuck.

We're both quiet on the way to school, but Paige smiles when she drops me off, and it's a real one. I'm in a daze as I walk the hall. When I get to my locker and open it, a folded piece of paper falls out. My name is spelled out on the front, and I recognize Isaiah's handwriting. I snag it and put it in my pocket until first period, so I don't have to explain myself to Becki or anyone else hovering nearby.

Once I get settled in my seat, I pull out the note and unfold it.

Library at lunch?

After everything that's happened with my experiments, I don't want to wait until science class to talk to Isaiah, so it would be good to meet him in the library. But it's tricky. I mean, he is Isaiah after all, and I like talking to him, but everyone thinks he's so weird, and Becki is probably already coming up with a fantastic name for me—something like "geek-lover." She'd say she's just teasing, but I'm not so sure. My stomach gets knotted up thinking about it. I don't like the way Becki can be, but I need something to stay the same. So, I need to figure out what to tell my friends. I tap my fingers on my desk. Isaiah and I *are* working on the project together. During the break after class, I tell Leah that I'm going to miss lunch because I have to catch up on our science project. Since she's the one who cares the most about homework stuff, she's the most likely to buy my story.

"Ugh, that stinks. Do you really have to meet during lunch?"

I'm prepared this. "It's either that or spend time after school. I figured this was better. Besides, we've got all night together, right?" I bump her with my hip, and she giggles.

I'm so relieved she's believed me that I'm not prepared for her next question. "So what's your project about?"

I forgot she has Mr. Sneed too, just during a different period. "Um . . . we're studying ghosts."

"For science?"

"Yeah. We're going to look at scientific theories related to their existence—how people try to prove they exist or whatever."

Leah stares at her shoes for a minute, while I watch her, wondering what she'll say. Then she links her arms with mine to start walking me to class. Just when I think I've gotten away with it, she leans in close. "Are you sure that's a good idea?"

I look over to see her face twisted with concern. "Leah, you know me and my ghost story stuff. It's just for fun."

"Are you sure?"

"Positive."

At least, I think I'm positive.

The library is open during lunch, but there aren't many people there. Technically you can't eat in here, but that doesn't stop people from trying. I wolfed down a peanut butter and jelly sandwich on the way here, but I do sneak in a bottle of water to unstick my tongue from the roof of my mouth. Isaiah waves to me from a table at the back of the room. I scan the area and am relieved when I don't see anyone I know. Not that I'm embarrassed to be seen with Isaiah. I'm not. Really. I don't care what other people say about him . . . do I? It's just easier when we have to be together in class. I don't have to worry about what my friends or anyone else thinks then. I know people shouldn't be so mean to Isaiah, and a part of me feels guilty for sneaking around, but it's like I lost my dad, too, when Mom died, so I can't lose everything at school, too. "What's up?" I ask as I slide into my seat.

"How are you doing today?"

"Fine. Why?"

"Andie, it's been a weird week, and you know it. One day you were upset and then yesterday you were so excited. I just know it's been hard."

"It's always hard, Isaiah."

"I know, but—"

"Really, I'm okay today. I started Operation Haunted House last night."

"You did? Already? What happened? What did you do?" He babbles as he begins to dig in his backpack. "You didn't use my chart. Why didn't you tell me you were going to start so soon?"

"I didn't think it mattered."

"Okay, well did you start with scents like you mentioned yesterday?"

I nod. "Why?"

"You didn't do anything else?"

"No. Would you tell me what you're talking about?"

"Here." He slides a piece of paper in front of me, and it's this very detailed list of potential experiments to try. There are blank spaces for observations. "This way, you can keep track of your results and figure out what's working best. And by documenting it, it just seemed more, well, scientific, I guess."

"Isaiah, I'm not doing this for the project."

"I know. But it's still *a* project—a bunch of experiments— and it just seemed like it deserves more structure."

For a second, I'm annoyed. But I study the chart, and I realize he spent all night on this. For me. And just like that, I love it so much I want to frame it and put it above my bed. Which I obviously cannot do. "Thanks. It's really cool."

He sits up straighter. "You're welcome. So, details, and you have to fill in the blanks now, please. Don't wait or your observations get stale."

"Stale observations? Are you like a forty-year-old man or something?"

He rolls his eyes. "I'm mature for my age."

I bet he gets told that a lot. The thing is, yeah, he thinks like an adult, but his energy is all thirteen-year-old boy. Minus the obsession with boogers and farts.

I pull out my pen and start making notes. I describe how Paige reacted last night. I note where I found my dad and then all the things Paige said and did this morning. I can tell he's trying to read as I write, and I'm going to tell him all of this anyway, so I angle the paper to give him a better view.

He talks to himself as I write. "Interesting. Oh. Huh. Really. Wow."

When I finish, I put the pen down, cross my arms, and say, "What do you think?"

"The plan is genius."

"Is it? Because I'm not sure it won't just make them feel worse."

"Andie, that whole sunscreen thing this morning—it's perfect. Paige took a positive cue from your mom. Or . . . from you, acting as your mom. Whichever. Isn't that what you want?"

It's reassuring, hearing it come from him. I wasn't sure if I was overreacting about it all. The only thing I don't mention is my mom's rings. I don't know. I just don't want to talk about that yet.

"So what's next?" he asks. "I've categorized by senses and time needed to prepare."

"I see that. I'm not sure. I'm not going to be home tonight, so I guess nothing until tomorrow sometime."

"Where?"

"Huh?"

"Where will you be tonight?"

"Oh, um, just to Becki's house."

The smile fades. "She doesn't like me much, does she?"

"She doesn't know you."

"No one likes me much, Andie."

I don't know what to say. We both know it's true, and I don't want to lie to him. "I do."

"Why?"

"What do you mean why? I just do." I attempt to change the subject. "So what are you doing this weekend?"

He shrugs. "Homework."

"The whole weekend?"

"Pretty much."

His tone is flat, but I can tell he's hurt.

"I'm sorry, Isaiah."

"Yeah, but not sorry enough to ask me to hang out, huh?"

He pushes away from the table, stands up, and walks away. I stare at the papers in front of me while my cheeks turn into fireballs.

Chapter Eight

Isaiah is not at our table when I walk into science class, which is not just unusual—I can't think of a time when he wasn't the first person in the room. I go straight to my seat and start setting up the experiment that Mr. Sneed has projected on the screen.

Isaiah arrives just before the bell rings, and he doesn't say anything when he joins me at the table. He hops right into the experiment and basically takes over. I feel really bad. I really like Isaiah, and I want to be his friend, but hanging out? How could we do that? I have so much going on between home and Becki, and I don't know if I could handle it if everyone made fun of me like they do Isaiah. I still catch people staring at me across the room with that "poor Andie" look on their face. Last fall, Becki was the one who told some girl to "take a picture; it'll last longer" and then grabbed my arm and pulled me away from the glaring expression. As awful as she's been, what would I do without her? But I'm scared of losing Isaiah's friendship, too. I'm afraid to open up the conversation again, but I know we can't work in silence forever.

"I really am sorry," I finally say.

He sighs. "I know."

"You must have *some* friends to hang out with."

"Not really. Just my little brother."

"Really?"

He shrugs.

"But, like, have you tried?" As soon as it comes out of my mouth, I realize he *is* trying. With me.

His brow crinkles, and I try to cover. "I mean, it doesn't make sense."

"I did try, when we first moved here three years ago. My mom even made me try a bunch of sports teams. That was a disaster." He snorts and keeps playing with this piece of paper, folding it over and over.

"What happened?"

He exhales loudly. "I'm sure you heard about what happened with Jeffrey and all those guys."

"Kinda." I try to make my voice soft, because I really want to hear what he has to say. Everyone at our school knows part of the story, but I'm not sure of all the details. Jeffrey Blaine is Mr. Washington Heights Middle School; they might as well give him a crown to wear around all day. My friends and I went to a different elementary school, but even we knew about

Jeffrey before we started at Washington Heights. I don't know a girl here who doesn't have at least a little bit of a crush on him. And everyone knows Jeffrey is the reason people avoid Isaiah. It's like Jeffrey put a curse on Isaiah, making it so people either hate him or treat him like he's invisible. Becki buys into it like everyone else does. "Jeffrey Blaine told me that kid is a monster and he'll go crazy in school." Whatever Jeffrey says, however he treats people, that's the law at this school. Jeffrey doesn't want us to like Isaiah, so most people don't. Only I've never heard why exactly.

"I might be smart in school, but I'm pretty dumb with people. My mom says I'm kind of like a puppy. I just get so excited. Anyway, I went to this super small private school before we moved here, so I didn't know a lot about how things worked. Like, I didn't know I couldn't just talk to people like Jeffrey. He started teasing me right away because I tried to sit near him at lunch the first day. No big deal, right? Anyway, he made fun of me all year."

"When was that?"

"Fourth grade. No jokes about being a fourth grade nothing, please."

He grins, but it's almost like a habit more than a real smile.

"Anyway, things didn't get really bad until my mom made me try baseball that summer. The funny thing is, I wasn't too bad, and I sort of liked baseball. I started to make some friends, and I even got invited to a birthday party that summer at the pool. Anyway, at this one game, Jeffrey was pitching for the opposing team. He kept saying stupid stuff about my hair and other things. Everyone on his team got in on it. Then I was at bat, and I don't know how it happened, but I hit the ball . . . hard . . . right at Jeffrey. It hit him in a bad place, you know?" He doesn't look up at me, and it takes me a second to figure out what he means. "Yeah. He doubled over and cupped himself. It's one of those things that's not really funny, but people laughed like on the funniest videos show. I guess then people were talking about it afterward too, and it really made him mad, so he started in on me worse."

"But you didn't mean to hit him!"

"He didn't know that."

"I still don't understand."

"I guess he started making stuff up. I don't know everything, but there was a story that I peed my pants once when I ran into him at the mall. Then school started, and that was that."

"That isn't fair at all."

He shrugs. There is an awkward moment of silence before he says, "Look, let's not talk about it anymore, okay? I just kind of got excited when you showed up at the library. I thought maybe this was more than just a school thing, but it's cool. I'll still work with you on the science stuff."

I'm hurt and relieved at the same time.

The whole afternoon, I think about everything but my classes. I study the schedule Isaiah made, hoping to make decisions about what the next step will be in the haunting. I know that it needs to be something that sends a clearer message, but does that mean leaving an item—like a hairbrush or a book—somewhere strategically, or does it mean leaving the TV on a specific channel?

I also think about whether or not to tell my sister about the rings I found. I'm sure she'd want to know, and I actually want to talk to her about them. But if I do, I'll have to tell her *how* I found them, and I'm not sure I want her to know I looked through Dad's drawers.

And I think about Isaiah. I try to imagine what life is like for Isaiah, and I feel so selfish. Here I go to group therapy and rip into Brian for only thinking about his own problems, but I've been working with Isaiah all year and it never occurred to me that he doesn't have any friends. I mean, I knew he didn't have a lot and that they probably weren't school friends, but I figured he must have some. He never seemed sad about it before.

It's so funny how much I want to talk to my mom about all this. Not funny as in fall down laughing, but weird funny. Like, I wouldn't have any of these problems if she were here, but, kind of like fixing my family, she's the only one who would know what to do about any of this.

I had been looking forward to the sleepover being a distraction from everything at home, but now that I'm here, I can't stop thinking about the project. And with everything else on my mind, I'm only half there, and it shows.

"Where are you tonight?" Leah asks.

"I'm here."

"Really? You're putting taco meat on top of your brownie."

I look down, and sure enough, my plate looks like an experiment in flavor mixing. I've also sprinkled cheese on my Jell-O. There's no pretending I wanted that.

"Oops," I say. Everyone laughs and thankfully they let me off the hook.

Everything's fine until we move on to truth-or-dare. I always used to like the silly dares. I can deal with things like "I dare you to kiss the fish tank" or "Double dare: call the pizza place and hang up." Now, especially, it's the truths I don't like.

The one that gets me tonight is, "Truth: do you like Isaiah— like *like* him like him?"

It should be easier to say "No way." It should feel less like a lie when I say it.

I don't think they notice. At least I hope not. It's not possible that I actually have a crush on him, is it?

"Duh," Becki says. "As if. Besides, Andie knows that if she ever dated a dork like that, I would unfriend her."

I get up to refill the popcorn to hide the reddening of my cheeks. I don't even know whether I'm embarrassed or angry. Why does Becki care so much about being popular? And why do I care what she thinks? It's not *that* weird to think someone could like Isaiah. He's sort of cute. He could use a haircut, and his clothes are usually too big, but he's got nice eyes and a great smile. Plus, he's really nice.

I'm relieved when Gisela suggests we watch a movie. Anything to end truth-or-dare. We make it an hour into *Pitch Perfect* before we attempt our own a cappella group, but we're really bad. Well, I am anyway. Before I know it, we're in the middle of a pillow fight. I laugh a lot, and for the rest of the night, I am a normal middle school kid. There is pizza and loud music and secret-telling, and, at least on the surface, all of our problems are put aside. For one night, I pretend I don't have secrets from them. I pretend I'm not worried about anything but having fun. If Becki tosses any other digs in my direction, I don't notice. Or maybe being together like this reminds us of how things used to be, and we all act a little more like we used to.

For tonight, anyway, there are no ghosts.

The next morning, I realize I forgot to tell anyone to pick me up. I try to call my sister, but she's at work. I tap my foot as I try my dad's number. He doesn't answer. I leave a message for show, but when I hang up, I turn to Becki's dad and lie.

"I think he's at work, too. I can walk. I don't mind." Her dad gives me a ride, but it smacks me back into reality. My mom would have picked me up. She wouldn't have let me go without talking to Becki's dad. Even then, she would have asked a lot of questions about what we would be doing. And she would have known what time to come get me.

I know my dad still loves me. He's just too lost to think about these things, and, really, it's not something he ever did in the first place. He doesn't even realize what's missing.

I let myself in and find the house empty. Since I don't know when my dad might come back, I have to be cautious about my strategy. I sit down on the couch in the living room, in the spot where I sprayed the cushion—my mom's spot. I need inspiration. I close my eyes and sink back into the seat. I let her scent hug me.

"Mom, I haven't talked to you in a while," I say softly. I hope she can hear me wherever she is. "Things aren't getting better, but you probably know that. I'm trying to do something here, and I'm not sure if it's a good idea, but I don't know what else to do. We all miss you so much. There are just so many things that you took care of and no one's taking over. We try, but we can't do it all, I guess. Anyway, I just wanted you to know that I'm thinking about you, in case you didn't know."

I inhale one more time and pat the back of the couch as I stand. Okay, so who needs a message more? Paige, or my dad? I suppose my dad would be the obvious choice, but I think I've made more progress with Paige so far. And Paige tries so hard to keep everything together. She deserves a little hope.

The other advantage is that I know she'll be at work until four, so I've got time.

Her room is spotless. It's so weird that her world can be completely upside down, but everything in her room still has its place. I haven't been in here for a while either. I guess we all keep to ourselves more these days. I can still remember all the times I used to sneak into her room to steal her toys or paper or whatever. She would stomp and scream and try to convince my parents that she should be allowed to have a lock on her door.

Like I did the other day in my dad's room, I take inventory.

Only one item sits on top of her dark purple comforter—a stuffed pig that she won at the county fair when she was eight. It was a really big prize for an eight-year-old to win, and she was so proud of it. So it stays with her no matter how old she gets. I bet she's won bigger prizes since, but they were never as special as Piggy.

Paige has a small desk that sits in the corner by the window. Just like her bed, there's not much clutter on it. A folder. An old plastic cup that holds pencils, pens, and highlighters. Above the desk, there's a huge corkboard that is probably the messiest thing in the whole room. It's jam-packed with all kind of pictures, old tickets, and postcards from places we've visited. There are also awards and ribbons, even an autograph from a Jonas brother—I don't know which one—that she got at some local "meet and greet" that my mom took her to. They stood in line for four hours, and my mom said *never again*, but Paige couldn't stop screaming and that made my mom laugh. I think my mom would have taken her a thousand more times. Paige obviously outgrew them, but she keeps just about everything that ever meant anything to her on that board.

Her dresser towers above the desk on its left. My parents picked it up at a garage sale when Paige was little, and they painted it pink with polka dots for her nursery. When Paige was my age, she finally convinced them she had long outgrown polka dots and pink walls. That's when the room was painted with the lilac and white stripes it has now. And they stripped the dresser and painted it white. The knobs became purple, to match the walls. The paint has chipped in a few places, revealing the old wood underneath.

Paige's jewelry box sits on top of the dresser. I know I shouldn't open it. She would kill me if she knew I was in here, let alone about to go through her things, but I have to figure out something different to help push Paige a bit. I open the top of the box, but it's pretty empty. My sister doesn't wear much jewelry. There's nothing with any meaning in here—just some earrings that probably came from Claire's.

I drop the lid shut and I wander toward her closet. I won't go digging, but I just take a quick peek. Nothing jumps out at me. Her closet is actually smaller than mine, but her room is a little bigger. Plus, I have to store our suitcases on the top shelf in my closet.

I back away from the closet and turn around slowly. I glance back at the bulletin board and then move over to it so I can see everything up close.

It's really become her scrapbook, only you can't see about half of what's up there because so much has been pinned to the board—there are layers and layers of items. I laugh at a picture of Paige's right ear. I think that's one of my mom's shots from when she was into photography for about a minute and a half. Apparently Mom thought she could do something with the lighting or the angle to make it look artistic, but it's just an ear. I lift up a sketch she must have done for art class—it has a big red A on it—and I see there's another one underneath it. The one on top is a still life of some fruit, but underneath is the portrait of a young woman. It looks just enough like Paige to be a self-portrait, only the face is distorted. The neck is as narrow as a straw, and the head is shaped almost like a diamond, with huge, bulging eyes and a wide forehead. In tiny letters at the bottom of the page, I see Paige's signature and a date. I flip back to the first sketch. Before. Before, there was normal, boring, expected still life. After, there was a messed up version of Paige with weird angles and nothing pretty. The teacher must not have understood the After, because above the distorted face, there's a red C- with a circle around it.

But I get it instantly. She feels like she's choking. She can't get enough air, but her head is so full it's about to explode. I feel exactly the same way some days. Like I've been cut off from the rest of my body and am about to float away.

As I lift the page corners, I catch a glimpse of another photo. I lift the drawings out of the way. Beneath them, a few pictures cluster together, held up by one yellow tack. I remove the tack carefully, pull out one of the snapshots, and slowly slide the tack back in place over the two remaining photos.

I set the snapshot on the desk, sit down, and stare at it for a while. For a few minutes, I feel as if I've been transported into the moment the picture was taken. It's from our vacation to California three years ago. The trip was full of ups and downs. It started out okay. We got to see a bunch of crazy stuff on Venice Beach, like a guy dressed up as the Easter Bunny, except instead of pants he had a tutu. My mom kept trying to get me to look away from the people who pretty much weren't dressed at all, but I snuck a couple of glances in. We also drove down to the San Diego Zoo. Then my dad got sick. We never figured out whether it was food poisoning or the flu. It didn't matter. For a whole day he was stuck in the hotel room—more like the hotel bathroom. But my mom was determined to keep the rest of us happy. She decided to take Paige and me to Disneyland by herself. Dad wasn't too interested in giant mice anymore anyway, and honestly, I'm not sure Paige was either. She sure didn't seem happy to be there. She'd been kind of moody the whole trip, although it was nothing we weren't used to.

"My hair looks stupid" meant that we had to wait an extra half hour for her to get ready.

"Ew, I'll get fat" meant that we had to walk an extra four blocks to find frozen yogurt instead of ice cream.

Stuff like that. The Disneyland day took the cake. Paige was all about showing off her teenage attitude. She snapped at mom about the littlest things. Nothing was right: The rides were dumb. The characters were for babies. My mom's face grew tired. A couple of times she lost it and told Paige to suck it up, but overall she stayed pretty calm. I'm not sure whether it was for my sake or her own. Either way, I was having a pretty good time despite Paige. My mom said later that it was us still having fun that led to Paige's tantrum. Yes, fourteen-year-olds can have tantrums. I hope I never do.

Paige stomped her feet. She screamed that she wanted to go home. My mom stood her ground in the middle of the sidewalk, right near a character spot where Peter Pan was signing autographs. I felt eyes staring at us. Some glared. My mom laughed. "That was a good one, Paige. Now, Andie and I are going to ride Space Mountain. You can either join us, or you can wait on that bench over there. If you move from this spot, you will be grounded for the next month, and you'll miss the final track meet."

That's how Paige got all these ribbons on her corkboard. Paige used to love track. Of course, that was Before. She quit the team before the season got under way this year.

Paige had plopped down on the bench and crossed her arms.

My mom and I literally skipped all the way to the roller coaster. She tickled me and we laughed. The line took forever, but we told jokes and talked about what else we wanted to ride. I always liked roller coasters, no matter how scared other kids were; I loved how they made my stomach flip.

By the time we got back, Paige appeared to have melted into the bench. We were still laughing when we got close. She stood up, sullen-faced.

"How was it?"

"Awesome!" I cried.

We moved on to the Haunted Mansion, which was pretty dumb, and when we got out, Paige whispered, "I should have gone on Space Mountain."

I saw my mom raise an eyebrow, and she glanced over toward me. Then she turned back to Paige. "What was that?" I loved it when my mom made Paige sweat.

"I should have come with you to Space Mountain. I've always wanted to ride that."

"Then why didn't you?"

"I don't know."

"Because you were being a brat?"

Paige sighed. "I guess so."

"So what do you propose?" my mom asked.

"Would you please ride it with me?" There wasn't a hint of sarcasm in Paige's voice.

"Are you prepared to actually have some fun?"

Paige rolled her eyes, but she smiled at the same time. "It might hurt."

"Yes, I'm sure it will, but it only stings for a minute. Come on."

I didn't really want to wait in another hour-long line, and I didn't understand what had just happened.

I didn't say anything until we had been in line about ten minutes. "Mom?"

"Yes?"

"How come Paige gets to ride now?"

"What do you mean?"

"I mean, didn't she make a bad choice?" I was ten, and my parents were obsessed with making the best choices.

My mom nodded slowly. "Yes, she did. But she realized her mistake and learned from it. You know, sometimes in life, we don't get second chances. There aren't always three strikes. But when it comes to me, you'll always get another chance." She wrapped her arm around Paige and kissed her on the cheek, causing Paige to shout "Ugh!" and rub the kiss off her face. But she was laughing the whole time.

As I stare at the three of us barreling down a track in Space Mountain, my heart swells. My face is contorted in one of those *this is awful/awesome* expressions. My mom looks bored. But Paige wears the biggest smile, and her hands are high above her head.

Yes, I think. *This is a message.* Careful not to be too obvious, I don't put the picture smack dab in the middle of the board. I tack it just off to the right of center. I let one of Paige's ribbons cover the top part of the picture on one side—it's only my head, anyway. Then I step back from the board. I turn around and close my eyes. I slowly rotate back and open my eyes. It's pretty subtle, but the picture is clearly visible now. I think she'll see it.

I hope she'll get the message.

Chapter Nine

Back in my room, the quiet rings in my ears. I pick up the ghost story I've been reading—I had hoped it might give me some inspiration. I read about ten pages, but I can't get into it. In the story, a girl's dog comes back as a ghost who can talk. The ghost dog takes on all the bullies who made the girl's life miserable. The girl squeals and jumps for joy every time one of the bullies runs screaming from a room or gets in trouble for claiming he saw a ghost. I try going under my bedspread and using the flashlight to read, hoping it'll make the story more exciting, like when I used to read them just for fun, but it doesn't help. I don't know. Maybe I won't be able to enjoy cheesy, unrealistic ghost stories anymore. Or maybe I'm just jealous.

I'd be happy to have my mom back in any form. She doesn't have to be a dog, even. She could be a rat, and I'd let my ghost rat follow me around. She wouldn't have to defend me or scare people with her beady red eyes. She'd just have to hang out and whisper words of encouragement sometimes.

In any case, in addition to being boring, this story doesn't give me any ideas for my project. I put the book down and rub my eyes. I haven't even been home two hours, and I'm already sick of being by myself. I figure I might as well attempt to work on our science project. I can't let Isaiah do everything, even if he'd probably prefer that I did. Besides, I'm curious. I want to learn more about the science of ghosts.

I skim the articles he's printed out, but they're so hard to follow, probably written by actual researchers who use words only other actual researchers can understand. I read the same sentence about five times before I give up. I decide to try another approach and carry my folder to my computer. I open up the web browser and type in "electromagnetic" and "ghost." A few of the articles had "electromagnetic" in the title, so I figure it must be important. The first hit is a Wikipedia entry that's mostly about ghost hunting. I gather this theory—that ghosts are made up of electromagnetic energy—is one of the most popular among the real ghost believers. They can use all kinds of strange equipment to measure paranormal activity. It's their "proof," so to speak. I already know a little about this from watching the ghost-hunting shows on television.

I keep reading, digging more into this theory. It turns out energy really is the base of most of the research about ghosts. I can't believe I'm studying thermodynamics on a Saturday. Just like with Isaiah's research papers, I barely understand what I'm reading. But Wikipedia makes some of it easier to figure out. *The first law of thermodynamics: Energy is neither created nor destroyed; it just changes form.*

I scratch my head, but if I'm understanding it right, I kind of like this theory. I can see why the wackos do, too. It actually makes sense in a way, at least what sense I can make of it. I read about how ghosts can actually use human energy sources, like draining a lightbulb. That could be interesting. That is, if either my sister or my dad had a clue that this theory existed. I could replace a live bulb every day with a dead one to make them think my mom was sucking the energy out of the room, but I don't think either of them would pick up on that message.

I get sidetracked from the science research as I read. I keep coming back to my other project.

I lose an hour exploring the five forms ghosts can be "seen" in: *orb, vortex, ghost-light, ectoplasm, and apparition.*

I try to figure out if there's any way to use this in my hauntings, but again, it's not really what I'm going for. I don't want my family to actually go crazier than they already are. I'm doing this to make them normal again. Seeing a ghost could definitely have the opposite effect.

It's getting late, and my eyes are blurring, so I stretch and head downstairs to see about dinner.

My sister sends a text saying she's bringing home food. She does that sometimes if someone had a bad order or a mistake was made, or sometimes the cooks are just nice and make extra. I hear the garage door and jump. It must be my dad. I wasn't planning to add any more "signs" to the house, but at the last second, I turn on the TV and flip through a few channels until I come across one that feels right. I'm smiling as I turn it off again and place the remote back exactly where I found it.

When I see my dad, my smile fades. His eyes are bloodshot, and he stumbles a little.

"Hey there," he says.

"Hey," I reply. "Where have you been?"

"Oh, you know, around."

"All day?"

I'm not sure why I'm pushing buttons. I kind of like to think it's something Mom would have done, though Paige is better at this than I am.

He reacts in slow motion. His eyes open wide as he appears to take in what I've said. He reaches a hand up and scratches his cheek.

"I had things to do, Andie."

"I bet," I say. And I turn to walk away. "By the way, Paige is bringing home food. You should eat it. It might help."

I don't know what I expect. Maybe I think he'll run after me or yell at me. I'm sort of disappointed when neither of those things happen.

My stomach grumbles as I walk away. *Please get home soon*, I beg Paige, even though she can't hear me. I need the food, but more than that, I need the buffer.

I don't get far before my dad catches up to me after all.

"Did you come home last night?"

"No, I had a sleepover at Becki's."

"You didn't tell me."

"I told Paige."

"Paige isn't your parent."

I try to swallow the bitter words, but they won't go down. "She might as well be."

His face crumples and he shuffles away. I hear him in the kitchen. It's times like this I get so confused. I can tell he knows what he's doing is wrong, but he doesn't change anything. I think he wants to. Otherwise, why would he be making coffee at five in the afternoon? I can smell it as it begins to brew.

I splash some cold water on my face and pick up my room a little until I hear Paige's feet pound on the stairs.

"Hungry?" she calls out from her room.

"Starving."

"I'm changing, but the food's on the table. Club sandwiches and pasta salad."

My belly flips in excitement.

My dad is a different man sitting at the table. His face still drags, but his eyes are brighter. He picks at some of the salad. It's the first I've seen him eat in a while. It shows in the deep hollows of his cheeks.

I grab a plate from the cabinet and then pause. Do I pile the plate up and head somewhere else to eat, or do I brave sitting at the table, given the fight we were about to have?

He answers for me, kicking at a chair with his foot as if to tell me to sit down. I slide in and dig into the three layers of sandwich so I don't have to talk. If it's a big enough bite, maybe I'll still be chewing when he's done stabbing his salad.

My sister trudges into the room. Her expression is tough to read. Her voice had been light just a minute ago, but now it weighs more somehow. "Is it okay?" she asks, pointing toward my sandwich.

I nod, and my dad mumbles, "Great, thanks."

"The pasta salad had to be tossed by tomorrow, and no one else claimed it. I love this stuff." She heaps spoonfuls into a bowl. "How was the sleepover, Andie?"

"Good," I say. "Same as always."

She hasn't made eye contact with my dad yet.

"What time did you get home?" she asks me.

"Around noon."

"Were you here?" Paige stares at Dad, who just shakes his head.

"What did you do, then?"

"Homework. I've got a big science project coming up."

Out of nowhere my dad asks, "Did you watch TV today?"

I steady my voice even though my heart is beating at the back of my throat. I'd never heard him turn it on.

"No, I was upstairs on my computer."

He takes a swig of coffee and then glances at my sister. "How about you?"

"I've been gone since seven thirty."

He nods and taps the table with his fingers.

A long, awkward moment follows. It feels as if the room has been put on pause.

It's Paige who pops the silence like a balloon. "I've been thinking a lot about Mom lately."

Just lately? I think. But she keeps going.

"I mean, obviously I'm always thinking about her, but lately I've been wondering what she'd think if she could see us now."

What if she can? I wonder. Laws of thermodynamics do a jig in my head.

We all know the answer to Paige's question, but no one wants to say it out loud. No one wants to admit that we're not exactly living life to the fullest.

Dad clears his throat and stops tapping. "You wanna watch a movie or something tonight?"

My eyes shift back and forth between him and Paige while my knee shakes under the table.

"Sure," she says slowly. "I don't have any plans."

I smile, but it's one of those no-teeth ones because I recognize the statement for what it is—an admission that things are wrong. Paige always used to have plans on a Saturday night. Mom would have noticed it, too. Either Dad doesn't or, like me, he chooses to ignore it because he has no idea what to say.

"Can we go to the store and get popcorn and Twizzlers?"

My dad reaches over and squeezes my shoulder. "Sure, Candy. Just let me hop in the shower."

After Dad heads upstairs, Paige and I clean up the kitchen. I feel like singing, but I suppose that would be too much, so I hum instead.

"Andie?"

"Hmm?"

"Do you ever wonder if Mom is trying to talk to you?"

I grip the plate I'm holding so hard I'm worried I might break it.

Chapter Ten

After she asks the question, Paige's cheeks grow red. "Um, well, I don't know. Why?"

"You . . . just . . . you're so into ghosts and stuff. I wondered if you thought she might still be around."

"I thought you didn't believe in all that."

"I know. I mean, I don't. I just . . . I don't know." She doesn't usually sound so tentative.

"Have you seen anything?"

"Oh, it's probably nothing. But I keep thinking I smell her, or things that remind me of her, and today I swear something in my room moved."

"What was it?"

"Nothing, really; just a picture."

"Huh, that's weird."

"I'm probably just imagining things."

"Maybe not. You know my science project?"

She nods.

"We're actually studying ghosts. There are a lot of people who think it's possible, and there are tons of theories about the hows and whys of it all."

"Do you buy into it? Do you actually believe it?"

I shrug. "I'm not sure. I don't really believe the crazy stuff and the scary haunting stuff like in those books I read, but the idea that the energy doesn't go away is kind of interesting to me."

Paige nods, but she doesn't say anything. Neither of us do for a while. I'm trying to figure out what else to say or what not to say.

She stares at her hands and whispers, "I hate him a little."

"It's hard not to."

Paige sighs. "But he just has a broken heart."

"I know."

"It's just that he's supposed to be the one who knows how to fix mine."

"I know," I say again.

It's quiet for a while as we finish putting everything away. I think about the rings. I know I can't mention my dad's room. She would guess that I'd been in her room, too. But I'm so curious. I really want to be able to talk to Paige about this.

"Do you know what happened to all of her stuff?"

"What stuff?"

"I don't know. Jewelry and personal things. It just feels like everything disappeared."

Paige tilts her head to the side. "Well, I think they buried her with some of it."

"Her wedding rings?"

"She was wearing them at the wake."

I nod. "I just wasn't sure if they took them off before they closed it."

She shakes her head. "Got me. I think you'd have to ask Dad about anything like that."

Things are quiet on the ride to the store. We aren't used to talking to one another anymore. Even small talk feels dangerous. I can't just say "How's the job hunt, Dad?" or "Do you think you could stay home more often?" We can't ask Paige about track anymore or about her friends or what she does for fun. I should have known that meant attention would shift to me.

"So, anything new in school, Andie?" Dad asks.

"Not really. I still hate math."

They both laugh. Paige turns around from the front seat. "I forgot to tell you. Your science partner came into the diner yesterday."

"Really?"

"Yeah, his mom left a big tip."

"That's good."

"He's nicer than you made him sound."

"What did I say?" I ask, a little sad that I might have made Isaiah look bad.

"Just how you were worried about being paired with the geeky kid."

My dad interjects, "Andie, that doesn't sound like you."

I bite my tongue so I don't say *"How would you know?"*

"I like Isaiah. He's okay. It's just that my friends don't."

"That's tough," Paige says.

I'm really surprised when my dad agrees. "Sometimes it's hard to deal with what your friends think. Especially at your age. I wasn't very good at it. I could probably still use some work on that."

"So, any advice?" I look out the window and watch the houses pass me by. The colors blur together.

"I guess just do the right thing."

"How do I know if it's right?"

"I think it pretty much comes down to this: listen to your gut. If doing what your friends want makes you feel like you're going to puke, it's probably the wrong thing."

"What if what makes me want to puke is ending up without any friends at all?"

They both go quiet. And, without either of them responding, I know I've hit a nerve. It suddenly occurs to me that they've both lost so many friends in the past few months that they might understand what I'm talking about.

When we get to the store, I find the microwave popcorn and some Twizzlers, and Paige chooses a big box of Whoppers. Dad even throws in a big bottle of Coke.

Back at the house, I toss a bag of popcorn in the microwave while Dad loads a movie into the DVD player. It's some classic sci-fi action flick thing. My dad insists it's the best of its genre and that we're in for a fantastic night. He can't believe we haven't already seen it. I whine a little but I don't care enough to protest much. I'm just glad we're all going to watch it together. I pour three glasses of Coke and Paige throws in a few ice cubes, then we carry everything out to the living room. Paige passes right by the couch. It's pretty clear she's avoiding it. Instead, she picks the hard chair that no one likes, opposite Dad's recliner. My dad eyes me on the couch. Instead of sitting in his usual spot on the recliner, this time he plops down next to me.

We only get about halfway through the movie before it starts skipping. By then I've noticed my dad is completely distracted by the smell of the couch. I sigh when the DVD finally stops working altogether.

"Want to switch it out for something else?" my dad asks.

My sister mumbles a *meh*.

"Whatever," I say. The moment is gone.

My dad mimics my sister's actions from the other night. He takes a long sniff of the air before getting up from the couch and heading to the kitchen. I hear a cupboard open and a glass clink against another, then the crack of ice. I listen carefully, hoping to hear water running; instead I hear the unmistakable sound of him grabbing a bottle from the top of the fridge. It's easy to recognize because the bottles hitting against each other make the kind of music that won't help you fall asleep at night.

Paige rolls her eyes and stands. "Well, that's that. I might as well go to bed early."

It's only eight, so I know she's not really going to sleep—she's escaping. I do the same.

Once I get to my room, though, I'm so bored I want to be anywhere but here. I try to read. I start obsessing. There must be more of my mom's things in this house. If my dad kept her rings, he probably kept some other things, too. While I'm considering where he would keep any of her things, I go back over the research from earlier. I even fill in the chart that Isaiah gave me. For a few minutes, I think about calling him. He wrote his number on top of the sheet. I even pick up my phone and run my fingers over the numbers. It would be so easy. I punch the numbers in, but I don't press SEND.

By nine, I'm wishing I had school the next day. How am I going to fill another day of this? I am so antsy that there's no way I'm going to be able to fall asleep right now. I give up trying, and decide to sneak downstairs. Maybe I can still attack those Whoppers. Paige barely touched them. Chocolate will help, right?

I grab the carton from the coffee table, and I wonder if my dad went to bed. I wander in the kitchen and see the empty glass in the sink. I open the garage door, and sure enough, his car is gone. I'm surprised I didn't hear him leave.

When I shut the door and turn around, I nearly run into the door to the basement, which somebody has left open. Ideas bang around in my head like a pinball machine.

Chapter Eleven

I turn on the basement light and then shut the door behind me. I go down the stairs slowly, almost afraid of what I might find at the bottom. The old rec room looks sad and lonely. We never really used it as a family room, but we used to have sleepovers down here, and for a long time it was also my toy room. It's still not "finished." It's just painted cement walls, a large carpet remnant, and a brown plaid couch my parents bought at a garage sale when they first got married. The couch smells as old as it looks. There isn't much else in here, so I pass through the large room and end up in the even more unfinished part of the basement.

When my parents bought the house, they always envisioned doing the basement up with nicer walls and ceilings and stuff, but at first they didn't have money and then they found out the basement leaks every time it rains. Even now the smell of must and mildew makes me gag. That's why everything stored down here is on shelves or in plastic bins. Nothing touches the ground or it gets ruined. They gave up redecorating after they got a quote for how much it would cost to fix the leaking.

I have no idea where to begin. It would help if any of the boxes were labeled. That's something my mom always said she'd work on, but it fell to the bottom of the list every year. I don't have a clue what's in most of these. I'm sure some of it's old baby clothes and stuffed animals. About five of the big plastic tubs are all the same size and shape. I open a lid and immediately see yellow baby blankets. They're bunched up and crammed into the box.

I let my eyes scan each row. There are a couple of red and green bins, and I think those might be Christmas decorations. Since they're on the top shelf, I don't check them. I start with the boxes on the lower shelves, cracking open each lid, mostly finding toys and games and other holiday stuff. One box is filled with a bunch of papers and artwork from when Paige was little.

All of this stuff has been here forever. Maybe this is a waste of time.

I stop what I'm doing and study the top shelves again, and finally something stands out. I see a hint of lettering on the side of one of the cardboard boxes. I can only see a couple of letters—NE—but they make my stomach flip. My mom's name is Diane, and the handwriting is very clearly my dad's large scrawling letters.

I take a step back and then turn and look for the small ladder we keep down here. It's tucked in behind the furnace, so I pull it out and put it right in front of the shelf with the box. I climb up a few steps and just get my fingers around the bottom of the box. I scoot it out toward the edge. I can tell already that it's pretty heavy, and I'm scared I'm going to drop it and all the contents will spill on the concrete floor. Worse yet, something will break, or my sister will come running because of the noise and I'll be busted.

I manage to get the box off the shelf and I grunt as I balance it on the top of the ladder. I take a breath and decide this is like ripping off a Band-Aid. I wrap my arms around the box and just go for it. My knees shake from the weight. I don't know if the box is too heavy or I'm not strong, but I set it down a little harder than I mean to just because I can't hold it up anymore. The crooks of my elbows have red marks where the lid dug into my arms.

I run my hand over the top of the box. I can feel my pulse beating in my thumb. Now, her name is clearly visible on the side of the box. I trace the letters with my finger. If there were ever a time for electromagnetic pulses or something, this would be it. I'd love to get a sign right now. A flickering light. The air-conditioning unit kicking in. Anything.

When nothing unusual happens, I lift the lid of the box. Suddenly I feel electricity, but not from an ectoplasm or anything like that. It's from me. It's like I'm lit up.

The box is full. At first glance, only a few items are visible. First, there's an old scarf that she made. My mom dabbled in sewing, but she wasn't very good at it. Every year for New Year's she'd resolve to improve. She'd buy patterns and fabric, and then she'd declare Sunday afternoons "me time." She set up a small space in the corner of the rec room part of the basement for her sewing table. Usually this phase lasted about two to three weeks. Just enough time for her to complete one project—something simple like a tablecloth or a scarf—decide that she would never be able to master it, and then toss the sewing machine into its box and tuck it back onto the shelf. I glance up and see the light blue container where she'd put it last January. Just a few days later, any chance that she'd become a seamstress ended.

That last time she pounded up the stairs and threw her hands up in the air, she'd announced, "Well, this is it!"

She had a hideous green and purple scarf tied around her neck. Not only were the colors awful, it was obvious that something had been put together wrong. One end was clearly thinner than the other.

Paige and I had glanced at each other, trying to figure out if it was okay to laugh.

"This is my masterpiece. What do you think?" my mom said before twirling around in a circle. I giggled first, and Paige burst out laughing.

"Yeah, yeah, you know you want one. But I'm afraid you're out of luck. I'm done sewing. For good this time."

"Oh suuuurre," Paige teased.

Just then my dad had come into the kitchen for a snack. He stopped and stared at her. "What's that?"

My mom had rolled her eyes and slapped him playfully on the arm. "It's a scarf."

He pursed his lips and nodded.

"Mom said she's done sewing," Paige announced.

"Oh yeah?"

"Yes, and don't try to talk me out of it." My mom held her hand up.

"But you have such natural talent," my dad deadpanned.

There was a pause before my mom's body started shaking, and I thought she was crying, but then she started giggling. Before I knew it we were all cracking up.

"Uh oh," my mom squeaked. "I'm about to pee my pants!"

She ran out of the room, still laughing.

Later, I asked her why she kept trying to sew as long as she did. "I always ask myself what I'd regret more," she told me, "wasting time trying or never trying at all. In the end, the answer's always the same. It's worth it to try."

I pick up the scarf and hug it to myself. At least she died without that regret. I wish this had been in the coffin with her. I'm glad the rings weren't, but this is the kind of thing that defined her.

My eyes drift back down to the box. I am a pirate, and this is my bounty. The chest is so full of treasure, I wonder if I'll ever be able to leave the basement again. I don't even notice the smell anymore. In fact, the only scent I take in comes from the box. I can't place it. It's not one of the top five smells on my list, but it makes me feel her around me. I sniff the scarf, but that's not where the smell is coming from.

The box is filled with things of all shapes and sizes. Nothing seems organized, but a lot of the stuff is in smaller boxes and some bags. The next thing I pick up is a plastic bag. It's folded around something, and I open it carefully. It's filled with greeting cards. I reach in and slide out a pink one. Big purple letters read *Happy Mother's Day!*

I don't remember this one. Paige wrote a nice message inside, but I apparently just scribbled something. There are Christmas cards and birthday cards, thank-you notes and Easter greetings. But at the very bottom, I see a stack of letters that have been tied together with pretty yellow ribbon. I gently pull on one end, holding on to the pile so they don't spill out on the cold damp floor. From the way they've been tied together, I can tell these are special.

They're all from my dad. A history of their relationship. Love letters. Anniversary cards. Some pictures of the two of them at special dinners. One from their honeymoon. My favorite is a picture he had taken of her when we went camping one summer. She sat at the edge of the lake. She must have just turned toward him or something, because she has a *What?* expression on her face. The light caught her blond hair at just the right angle, and she almost looks like an angel.

I turn the picture over. In that trademark scrawl, my dad had written, *This is the reason.*

For what? I wonder. It's like they were having a conversation. It must have been a good answer to an important question for her to tuck it in this pile.

At first I'm surprised my dad would hide all of these treasures down here in the basement. Why wouldn't he want them close by? Wouldn't he want to see them? To remember?

But then I remember his tantrum in their bathroom, and I think more about what these cards really say. He loved her so much. Probably even more than I ever knew. Maybe even more than she did. He was definitely more romantic than I would have guessed. It instantly reminds me of the person he used to be. Maybe he did lose more than my sister and I did. We talk about losing a parent like it's the worst thing in the world, and for me it is, but maybe it's worse for him. Not worse exactly, I guess. Just different.

I keep thinking of all the things my mom will miss out on in my life—high school and boyfriends, proms and graduations, weddings and babies. But that's the thing. I still live my life, going forward to the very things my dad thought were settled. Weddings and babies. This is his life, and maybe it feels less like something is missing from it for him, and more like it's actually over.

It's such a heavy thought, my head falls. I'm not sure I want to keep looking. My dad packed these memories away for a reason. Maybe he had the right idea—it's like a lake. Shimmery and smooth like glass on top, but if you start to dredge, everything gets murky and nasty.

I'm considering shutting up the box when my eyes are drawn to a bright pink string. I have to move a few things to see that the string draws a cloth bag closed. Reaching in, I figure out what the scent was; a crumpled dryer sheet falls out when I lift the bag up. No surprise. I swear my mom put them in everything. She liked the way they smelled, so she used them like an air freshener.

Inside the bag, I can see the outlines of books, and the bag is so heavy that I have to use both hands to pull it out. When I tug loose the opening, I still have no idea just how valuable this box is.

Chapter Twelve

I gently open the first book I pull out, and I see two dates: June 8, 1999, and September 16, 2011. The first date is written in black marker and the second in blue ballpoint pen. I turn a page, and the next is filled with her tall cursive loops. I read the line across the top: *Andie just turned one, so naturally, I'm going insane and loving every second of it.* My eyes burn with tears. I close the book before any fall on the page.

How did I not know these exist? My hands shake and my heart seems to be trying to escape my body by jumping out of my throat. My mom kept journals. Most of them are identical brown Moleskine books. I try to count, but my brain can't even handle the simple math. There's a bright pink one with daisies and another that's covered in green and blue stripes.

All of the bacon in the world has nothing on one sentence of her words. I feel like my mom is sitting right here with me.

I'd almost forgotten what her voice sounded like, but now it sings in my ears, making my whole body dance.

What do I do with these? I can't read them all down here. I know I shouldn't take them upstairs though.

I know I shouldn't.

I work fast, putting all of the journals back into the bag, then setting the bag down on the ground beside me and closing up the box. It's much lighter now without the journals, easier to push up to the top shelf. After returning the ladder back by the furnace, I hug my precious cargo and tiptoe back up the stairs. Glancing at the clock on the microwave in the kitchen, I discover I've been down there longer than I thought. It's three thirty in the morning. Just as I shut the basement door behind me, I hear the garage door start to open. I gasp and run as quietly and as quickly as I can to my room. I shut the door behind me, turn out the light, and hop into bed, still clutching the bag of journals. I tuck them in beside me and pull my covers up to my chin. My breath comes fast and my heart beats like a woodpecker.

Maybe he didn't notice my bedroom light was on when he pulled up.

But of course he did. He doesn't notice there's no food in the house until a social worker tells him about it, but at three thirty in morning, he decides to be observant.

A soft rap on my door makes me jump, even though I know it's him. "Andie?" His voice is soft, cautious, almost like he hopes no one will hear him.

"Yeah?"

The knob turns, and he peeks his head in. "Are you okay?"

"Yeah."

"Why are you up so late?"

"I couldn't sleep, so I did homework."

"You sure you're okay?"

It's dark, but light floats in from the streetlamp outside, giving his face a soft glow. He doesn't look drunk.

"I'm fine. Really."

"Well, you should get some sleep."

"Okay." He starts to close the door. "Dad?"

"Hmm?"

"Are you okay?"

I hear him exhale, but he doesn't come back into the room. "I'm working on it."

Once the door shuts, I lean over and grab the flashlight from the drawer of my nightstand. I'm used to reading all kinds of half-stupid and half-scary stories under these covers. I read because I can't sleep, and then they freak me out so I really can't sleep. Tonight, though, I read an actual ghost's story.

I don't like the freshly mobile stage in toddlers. I didn't enjoy it with Paige either. Of course, that makes me feel guilty. Aren't moms supposed to love every stage? Aren't I supposed to clap and cheer at every milestone? But during this stage, I feel like I lose my freedom, hence my sanity.

Even with the pretty loops and her voice in my head, I have a hard time picturing her writing these words. How could my mom have felt that way about Paige? About *me*?

I can't leave her anywhere, nor is it easy to take her places. I get it. They just want to move at this stage, and they become outrageously frustrated if they can't, but I miss plopping her in a Pack 'n' Play so I could shower or make a phone call or pay a bill.

What if these don't get better? What if I have hundreds of pages of my mom complaining about being a mom? I don't know if I should read more.

But I can't not read more.

If I complain, Dave—the original Mr. Fix-It—says, "You can go back to work." But he doesn't understand. That's not an option, because as hard as it is to be with her all day, not being with her would be a thousand times harder. There's nothing quite like being the center of her universe.

Oh, there she is. Relief washes over me, and I smile. That's my mom.

My eyes droop. I never want to stop reading, but sleep wins the battle. I tuck the book back in the bag and put the whole thing under my bed where no one will see it. I drift off into dreams of laughing babies and lullabies.

My eyes pop open at ten. For a second I wonder if I imagined everything from last night, and I roll over and reach under the bed. When my fingers feel the cloth, I sigh with happiness. I want to rip open the bag and read them all right now, all day without ever stopping, but my stomach growls and I have to pee, so I toss the covers off and race to the bathroom. When I go downstairs, my dad is watching television, back in his usual recliner.

"Hey there," he says.

"Morning."

"You must be tired today."

"Nah, I'm okay. Just hungry."

He nods, and I rush into the kitchen, grab a Pop-Tart and a glass of juice, and hurry back toward the stairs.

"So what's on your agenda today?" my dad asks as I pass by. I pause with my food in hand and shrug.

"You want to go see a movie today? Since we failed with *Dune*?"

I can honestly say that before I went to the basement, the idea that I might be faced with the dilemma of spending time with my dad or reading my mom's journals would have made me happy, but I'm torn. On one hand, I can't give up this chance with my dad. Isn't that what I've wanted? Him to be normal again? But my mom's words? I need them.

My indecision must register on my dad's face because he says, "It's no big deal if you've got something else to do."

It's his face that seals the deal. "A movie sounds good, Dad. What time?"

He reaches forward to the coffee table where the thick Sunday newspaper lies neatly piled. "I have the times right here. Looks like there are a couple of good options around twelve thirty or again around three."

Inside I dance a crazy jerky happy dance. "How about three? I've, um, got to work on my project for school. I was thinking about going to the library, and they close at two on Sunday anyway."

I tell him I'll walk, and he agrees to pick me up so we can go right to the theater. I start to take the stairs two at a time, but my juice spills, so I slow down. I eat and get ready in a flash. Then I take out all of the ghost research in my backpack and replace it with the entire bag filled with journals. There are a lot of them, but I want them to stay together, like somehow she's more whole if I have all the journals in one spot. Plus, I don't know where to start. I like knowing I can pick a different one if I come across a bad year or something. It makes my backpack heavier than usual, and I groan when I throw it on my back. It's going to be a long walk to the library, but it'll be worth it. No interruptions. No fears of getting caught.

This secret on my back weighs me down. Not just because it's heavy, but because not being able to share it makes it feel like it's wrong. It can't be, though, can it? Bringing my mom back into this house is already helping, isn't it?

Before I leave the house, I decide I need to escalate things. My dad and Paige need more. I want more.

My dad has set me up and he doesn't know it. His iPod is on shuffle, plugged into the speakers in the living room, and I can hear his shower running upstairs. *Please let it still be on there,* I beg as I scroll down. He's purged so much, there's a good chance it won't be anymore, but I pump my fist when I find the playlist I hoped for. My mom made it for their last anniversary. It's a list of songs that reminded her of him. He thought they'd be all sappy and romantic, and a few were, but she also mixed in some humorous ones, like some old country song about how hard it was to be humble when you're perfect.

I press play and duck out of the house before he gets out of the shower. As I'm closing the door, I hear this old song, "I'm Too Sexy," filling the house with a different kind of ghost: the memory of laughter. My dad used to dance around the house in his robe and slippers lip-syncing. Paige would roll her eyes and groan. My mom would pretend to be mortified, but eventually she'd give in and double over laughing at him.

Chapter Thirteen

My favorite corner of the library is in the teen section. Yes, I have a favorite place in the library. My mom brought me here a lot. It usually kept me quiet and busy for a little while.

No one comes into this corner. It's far from the windows, so it's a little darker than the rest of the room, and instead of the big, brightly colored beanbag chairs scattered throughout the rest of the teen section, this corner has an old-fashioned high-back chair with red and orange flowers all over it.

A sign above the chair reads Ms. Foster's Nook and goes on to explain that she was a major benefactor to the library. A long time ago she used to read to kids in this chair or something, and they had to keep it. But obviously they didn't want it on display in the front of the library or anything. I always thought it was kind of sad how Ms. Foster got pushed to a back corner. Out of sight, out of mind. They got what they needed from her, I guess. The chair wasn't the most comfortable one, but it always felt like the right place to read a book.

Once I'm settled into the chair, I open my backpack and pull out the bag. Just seeing all the diaries makes my toes tingle, like all the excitement is running through my body and it has nowhere to go but my feet. I'm faced with my second dilemma of the day. Where do I start?

I opt for the grab-bag approach, closing my eyes, reaching in, and pulling out a random Moleskine.

Flipping open the front cover, I find I've grabbed the same one I started reading last night. Okay, I get it. I'm supposed to read this one.

Once I start, my eyes don't leave the page until I've practically memorized each and every word. The entries are sporadic. Sometimes she writes every day for several weeks in a row, and then six months pass before the next entry. A couple of the entries are only a paragraph long, or even just a sentence, describing her general mood or the passing of an event. *Busy with Paige's school these days* or *Celebrated another anniversary.* Many are pages long, like once she got started she couldn't stop. Mostly, the entries are just babble, really, and I'm sure it would bore most people, but I love it. It's like watching a video recording.

Which makes me stop and think: we have video somewhere, don't we? We must. I know my parents hadn't been as good about pulling the video camera out over the past few years, really probably since Paige got old enough to run and hide every time she saw a camera coming, but still, there must be some. I make a mental note to search.

The last entry is tough to read. It's sad. This journal ended just a week after 9/11. Mom describes what it felt like to watch the news, how hard it was to envision raising a child in this world. That's not the hard part though.

It reminds me how quickly things can change. I always worry about losing my kids—doesn't any parent? But watching the towers fall reminded me that I, too, am just as vulnerable. Dave and I haven't updated our wills in ages, but I've put in a call to a lawyer. I went back through some of my journals and I realized I'm not saying much here. Maybe I need to try harder to leave something for the girls, just in case. But what do I say? What would someone want to hear if they lost a loved one too soon? Is it ever not too soon? Anyway, this is what's keeping me up at night these days.

Suddenly, I can't catch my breath. Her words press down on my chest, and I have to stand and walk around to get any air. She didn't know. She couldn't know. No one does; but she'd thought about it. She'd worried about it.

I think about that statement: *Is it ever not too soon?* Yes, I think, definitely. If she were ninety it wouldn't have been too soon, right? Or maybe it would have been, but I sure wouldn't have minded waiting to find out. I pull out my phone to check on the time. I still have about an hour before Dad will pick me up. I can read another one, but I'm torn. I want the words to last forever. Maybe it's like a pan of brownies. I usually eat them so fast, and I'm disappointed the next day when they're all gone. I should savor these. A few here and there. Let them last for months and months.

I feel selfish. I should share these with Paige, right? I know she would want to see these. She deserves to, but I don't feel like I can do that until my experiment is over. I don't want to risk her figuring out that I'm behind everything.

I start pacing the small hallway next to the chair. You're not supposed to talk in the library, but it's deserted back here. Plus, it's Sunday afternoon in the teen section. No one's around. I pick up my phone and scroll through the numbers. I put Isaiah's number in last night. I don't know why he's the one I want to talk to so much. I scroll back through until I see Gisela's name.

I'm relieved when she doesn't answer. Weird.

I don't even think as I hit call again. Isaiah's answered the phone before I even register what I've done.

I hesitate, not sure what to say. "Um, it's me. Andie."

"I know who it is, silly."

"Oh."

"What's up?"

"I don't know."

"Ooo-kaaay." There's a long, awkward silence.

"I found my mom's journals."

Another silence, but this one isn't awkward. I can hear his breathing. I know he's just patiently waiting for me to say more. A few seconds later, I launch into the whole story of the weekend and everything that's happened. I tell him about the rings and the words and the smells. He doesn't say anything.

When I run out of things to say, I exhale. "That's it."

"I see," he says. "That's a lot to take in."

"Yeah. I'm starting to feel confused. Should I stop the experiment and talk to my dad or Paige?"

"I don't know, Andie. It seems to be working."

"Maybe."

"If you tell them now, and things go back to the way they were, you'll never be able to try this again."

"I know. So you don't think I should."

"Maybe not yet. But it's a tough choice."

"Isaiah?"

"Hmm?"

"Thanks for listening."

"No problem. Really."

"I better go. My dad will be here soon, and they'll be closing the library."

"You're at the library?"

"Yeah. Why?"

He laughs. "Because I'm sitting on the front steps. I was working on homework."

"Stay there."

I collect my books and walk/run as fast as I can to the front door. Isaiah is sitting on the steps, wearing a red polo and khaki shorts. It looks like a school uniform. But I'm happy to see him. I call out his name as I pass through the front door.

He stands up, and I jog to him, and then stop short. We're only a few feet apart, and now it's weird. I kind of want to hug him, but that would be *super* weird.

"Are you leaving?" I ask.

"Yeah, my mom's on her way."

We wait on the steps in silence until his mom pulls up. She leans out the window and waves at me. "Need a ride?"

I shake my head. "My dad's coming." I feel so proud to say it. So normal. And I actually believe maybe things could be again.

Twenty minutes later, after I've tried to call my dad three times and texted him twice, I realize how wrong I was. As I pull my straps over my shoulders and start the trek back home, I wonder if disappointment is the new normal.

When I get home, I find him sleeping on the couch. Maybe passed out.

I stomp my foot and huff. Then I kick the basket of afghans next to the couch. He still doesn't move, so I yell "Thanks a lot!" and then run up the stairs. Either he doesn't hear me or he doesn't know how to respond, because I don't see him again all afternoon. At dinnertime, I find a note on the kitchen table.

Sorry about the movie, Andie. I fell asleep. Maybe next week.

Right.

I'm so mad I grab a pillow and scream into it. I really thought things were going to change. Things have to change. I sit up in my bed and pull my phone out of my pocket.

Isaiah is short of breath when he answers. "Hey."

"He didn't come."

"How'd you get home?"

"I walked, but that doesn't matter. I don't know what to do. What am I doing wrong?"

"I don't know."

"Isaiah, you're the smart one. Help me figure it out."

He doesn't answer right away. I can hear him breathing though. His voice is thin and tentative when he speaks. "Maybe it's time to stop. I'm a little worried about you. My mom says—"

"What did you tell your mom?"

"Nothing. I mean, not about the project or anything, Andie. Just that things had been hard. Anyway, she asked if you had ever been to see anyone as a family. Like Mrs. Carter, but not Mrs. Carter. A real psychologist."

I'm gripping my phone so hard my hand hurts.

"Never mind," I say, trying to keep my tone light. "I'll figure something out. Thanks for listening."

"Andie, don't—"

"I gotta go. Still have some other homework to do. Talk to you tomorrow."

When I end the call, my brain goes into overdrive. Anything to avoid thinking about what he said. I focus on what happened with my dad.

What caused him to change again so quickly? Was it the music? What's the pattern here? Paige seems to respond almost instantly to the signs of Mom. Her entire mood shifts. Dad is hit or miss. More miss than hit, actually. And it's almost like the reminders hurt him more than they help.

I look for patterns, and I come up with a possibility. He needs direct messages. He always has. It's right there in Mom's journals. He's Mr. Fix-It, but he avoids real problems. Everything I've tried so far—the body spray, the iPod—they're too subtle. They remind him but they don't tell him anything, whereas Paige so desperately wants a sign that she hears the message right away.

I have to work on them differently. I fall asleep trying to come up with a new plan.

Chapter Fourteen

Monday morning talk is all about two things: boys and the upcoming rec night.

Becki is obsessed with Gavin Dolan. "Do you think he'll be there? What should I wear?"

Gisela smiles. "Definitely a dress."

"No way," Leah says. "Go casual. Otherwise you look like you're trying too hard. Plus, you want to be able to play the games."

I laugh with everyone else until Becki turns to me. "Do you think Isaiah will be there?"

She says it with a singsongy voice, clearly teasing me. I kind of feel like she just pulled my hair or something. Why would she bring that up?

"I don't know."

"Oh come on, admit it, you *liiike* him." Then she makes a face with her tongue sticking out.

I sigh. "Whatever."

I want to get up and leave, but I can't let her know she's getting to me. That would just make her tease me more. A few minutes later the first bell rings, finally giving me permission to head off to my locker. Gisela catches up to me. "I'm sorry."

I shrug. "What's up with her?"

"I'm not sure. I think she's kind of stressed out."

I roll my eyes. Stressed. She doesn't know stressed.

"Anyway, I know it's not very nice." She pulls her book bag up tighter on her shoulder and tucks her curly brown hair behind her ear.

"Yeah," I say, staring at my feet.

"Are you okay?"

When I look at her face, her eyes are so open. She looks like she really wants to know. I take a risk. "Sort of. I mean, things have been pretty cruddy at home, but I'm trying to make things better." I pause. "Can I tell you a secret?"

"Sure." She pushes her hair back behind her ears and tilts her head to the side.

"I found the coolest thing this weekend. My mom kept journals. I haven't told anyone in my house I found them yet. I sort of want to keep them to myself, you know?"

She bites her lip and nods. "I guess."

"Plus." I lower my voice and lean in. I feel pretty sure this plan is working, and I'm exciting to have some good news to share with Gisela for a change. Still, I drop my voice so no one else hears. "I'm doing a kind of experiment on my family that seems to be helping. I'm sort of making them think my mom's ghost is around."

"Huh?" Her eyes go wide and then narrow. I realize how crazy I must sound.

"Not like that. Not really. Just little things. Like, a song playing on the radio, or a scent in a room."

"What? Why?"

"Well, I think it's helping, actually."

"Helping with what?"

I glance at the clock. We only have a few minutes. "We've been kind of falling apart. I think my mom can put us back together."

"You could talk to us, you know," she says. "How bad has it been?"

There's definitely not enough time to answer that question, so I shrug.

"Are you sure you're okay?"

"That's a much tougher question than you'd think," I say. "But it'll get better."

Gisela gives me a small smile and squeezes my arm. The bell rings again, and I race to class.

I have an individual session a couple of times a week. At least it's not group, and it gets me out of gym, which means no stinky locker room for me today. Whoo hoo!

Usually, Mrs. Carter waits for me with an open door and a big smile. Today, I meet a closed door. Did she forget? Maybe after last week she decided she doesn't want to do the one-on-one sessions either. I knock a few times and wait. I hear a faint "*Come in*" and I turn the knob slowly.

Mrs. Carter is sitting at her computer, with her back toward me. I pause for a second while she hammers away at the keyboard. "Do we, um, have a meeting today?" I ask.

The typing stops. She glances at the clock, then swivels around to face me. "I wasn't sure you would show up."

My brow crinkles, and I suck in my lower lip. Despite what happened last week, I've never been good with confrontation.

"I thought I was supposed to be here."

She sighs. "Andie, you're not required to come, you know. I want you to show up each week because I think it's good for you. But obviously you've been holding back. I thought you might have decided our sessions weren't helping you."

Oh, well played, Mrs. Carter. I love how she twisted that around and put it right back on me. She's always good about that when I'm trying to figure stuff out with her.

"It was a bad day."

"So I gathered. There might have been more effective ways to deal with that bad day than to take it out on Brian though."

She motions toward the chair next to hers. Keeping my head low, I slide into it.

"Honestly, Mrs. Carter, I think he kind of deserved it." I don't look up when I say it, so I have no idea whether she's able to keep her face as open and friendly as it usually is.

"Do you believe people deserve to have their feelings hurt?"

"I'm not sure that's fair. He hurts our feelings all the time; he just never notices. He acts like none of us have real problems and goes on and on about his. I know I blew up, but maybe he needed to hear it."

"I see. So, are you admitting then that you have real problems? Because I was under the impression that you were fine; it was everyone else who was having problems adjusting."

Dang, maybe she's better than I thought. "I never said that."

"Not exactly, but you talk a good deal more about the problems your father and your sister are having than you do about your own feelings."

"What's going on with them sort of is my problem."

"Most certainly, but it's not your only problem, is it?" My dad's words swim through my head: *Let's just keep our problems to ourselves, okay?* Should I trust her anymore? Suddenly she seems sneakier than I'd remembered.

"Why did you call my dad last week?"

"To ensure you were safe."

"But I thought you weren't going to share anything we talked about with him."

"You know we don't have the same confidentiality agreement as a regular doctor and patient, Andie. This was serious, and our group session wasn't the only indication I had that things had escalated at home."

My head snaps up and I glare at her. "What do you mean?"

"Other people are concerned about you, sweetie. Teachers and friends."

Stupid growling stomach. It had to have been my math teacher. But friends? Who? My mind instantly settles on Isaiah. He told his mom that things were bad at home for me. What exactly *did* he tell her? I'm an idiot for trusting him. Becki was right; he's just a geek and there's a reason he has no friends. Everything suddenly makes sense. I know exactly why he can't keep friends. He isn't trustworthy.

Mrs. Carter interrupted my thoughts. "Are you ready to share more about how things are at home?"

No. But I shrug. "It's been better."

"Why do you think that is?"

"Maybe your phone call? I thought what we talked about here was between us!"

She settles back in her chair and runs a hand through her hair. "Hmm, so you think my contacting your dad is a problem. Is that the only reason things aren't going well?" The question weighs too much; it must be loaded with something. Everything's gotten too complicated, and I don't want Mrs. Carter's help anymore. I can't tell her anything more about my dad, but I don't know how to lie either. I just want her to leave me alone. I feel like I'm trapped in a microwave. It's small and hot, and the only escape is for someone to press the button and open the door. I'm turning around and around, getting dizzy.

"Andie, are you haunting your family as your mom's ghost?"

Isaiah told her *everything*.

I feel like I've been ambushed, and now I'm boiling over. I want to pick up my chair and throw it against the wall. But

I need Mrs. Carter to back off. I need her to think I really am *just fine*. So I form a tight smile. "Huh? I don't know what you mean."

"Have you been doing things to make your family think your mom is trying to communicate with them?"

I shake my head. "No."

"Please don't lie to me. A friend came to me very concerned that you might be doing something unhealthy."

"I don't know what you're talking about. Really." I hate Isaiah. I hate him so much right now. "I wonder if maybe that person is confused." I guess if she's not going to name names, I won't either. "My sister smelled something that was like my mom's perfume the other day and she saw a picture that made her feel like she should be trying harder. Just stuff that happened."

For a second she stares at me. She's waiting for me to break. I don't. She is going to have to be the one to give in. "You're sure. Because your friend was pretty certain."

"I'm sure. I'm sure my *friend*"—*ex-friend*, I think—"just misunderstood what I was saying. Everyone knows how into ghosts I am."

This seems to actually convince her. Even Mrs. Carter knows about my love of ghost stories. We've been meeting for months, and sometimes I don't want to talk about the hard stuff.

I'm in a daze when I leave her office. I'm so stupid. How could I have trusted Isaiah? During lunch I march into the library. I spot him instantly, his eyes trained on a computer screen.

I get close, kneel down next to him, and whisper in his ear, "Not cool, Isaiah. I don't know what you were thinking, but no wonder you can't keep friends."

He looks like someone kicked his puppy as I stand up and walk away before he can speak.

I'm shaking too much to join everyone at lunch right away, so I end up in the bathroom, where I splash cold water on my face. It does nothing to cool my raging temper.

By the time I meet up with my friends outside, there are only a few minutes left until the bell rings for class. I'll have to face Isaiah again in science, but at least he'll know that I know and won't try to talk to me. I hope.

Becki, Leah, and Gisela are huddled in a tight semicircle. Their heads are bent close together and they're whispering. They might as well be a poster for middle school mean girls—except, they aren't the mean girls. I know I'm interrupting something though, because Gisela and Leah stop talking the minute I approach. But Becki's back is toward me. Leah waves her hand in front of her throat trying to get Becki to stop talking, but it's too late. I hear her say, "It'll be fine, Gisela. You did the right thing."

"Did the right thing about what?" I ask as I complete the circle. Becki takes a step back, changing the shape of the circle to more of an oval. Leah follows suit. Gisela doesn't move, and she stares at her feet.

Becki tosses her hair and smiles at me. "Oh nothing. Just a stupid class thing."

Gisela looks up briefly and smiles, but it's a weak one.

Leah steps forward and puts her arm around me. "How are you doing?"

I feel my eyebrows rise, and I tilt my head. "Fine. Why?"

"Well, Andie, we know that—"

Becki cuts her off. "She's fine. Just look at her."

The whole thing is so weird. I don't know why I'm so dense, but it doesn't occur to me until we are about to walk back into the school that someone other than Isaiah could have told Mrs. Carter. In the space of like ten minutes, I completely forgot that I'd told someone else what was going on.

I've been betrayed by the person I trusted more than anyone.

The four of us are walking in pairs. Leah stays by my side, and I suddenly stop.

"What's wrong?" she asks, turning to face me. Becki and Gisela keep walking. They must not have heard.

"It was Gisela."

"Huh?"

"Did Gisela talk to Mrs. Carter?"

Leah doesn't answer, but she doesn't have to. The panic on her face is all the response I need. I leave her standing there and try to catch up to Gisela and Becki, but it's no use; they've already been folded into the crowd.

And now I dread going to science class and facing Isaiah for a whole new reason.

Chapter Fifteen

He's not there.

And I want to throw up.

I don't see him the rest of the day.

The nausea never goes away.

I avoid Gisela. After lunch I was desperate to confront her, but the rest of the day I just worry about Isaiah, and I don't want to see her. I can't handle what she did to me. Why would she do that? She didn't even get all the information. She just jumped to a conclusion.

Which, of course, is what I did, too. As mad as I am at Gisela, I'm madder at myself. And I'm mad at my other friends, too. All this time they've been trying to ignore what's happening with me, and then, instead of helping me, they go behind my back? And try to cover it up?

Who are my friends, anyway?

I look for Isaiah after school, but it's pretty clear he must have gone home early, which makes me feel even worse. I pull out my phone as I start to walk toward home and try to call him, but he doesn't pick up. I don't know what to say on a message, so I don't bother to leave one.

My phone buzzes a few minutes later, and when I look at the name, my shoulders slump in disappointment. Not Isaiah. It's Gisela.

I'm so frustrated that I can't talk to Isaiah that I pick up. She should know how mad I am.

I can barely understand her through her tears. "I'm so sorry if you're mad at me, but I'm worried about you."

I let her blubber for a few minutes, and then I say, "Is that it?"

She sniffs. "Are you mad?"

"What do you think?"

"What's going to happen? You know, with Mrs. Carter."

"Hopefully nothing. Do you understand how serious this is? Do you want my family to fall apart and for me to end up in foster care or something?"

She stammers a no.

"Okay, then just leave me alone. You took what I said and made a way bigger deal out of it than you needed to. It may have really messed things up, but I think I got it worked out for now."

"But, Andie, you sounded so weird. This isn't normal."

"Do you think you could have talked to me about it first? Given me a chance to explain more? No, you just went and blabbed."

"I didn't know what would happen."

"No, because you didn't ask. No one does. You know, today was the first time anyone actually asked me how I was doing, and Leah only did it because she was trying to cover up or felt guilty or something."

Suddenly, I hear Becki's voice instead of Gisela's. "Andie, you don't need to be so mean to her. She feels bad enough. We understand things aren't good, and we feel terrible that your mom died, but we can't talk about it all the time."

Her words are like ice. They cool me instantly in a way I didn't know was possible.

"Yes, yes, you're right. We can't talk about it all the time. Or at all, really. It might interfere with time spent talking about more important things like nail polish colors or stupid boy bands. I can see why it would be a problem. Don't worry, I'll make sure you never have to think about my dead mother again."

Then I press the end button. I try Isaiah's number again. Voice mail. This time I leave a brief message because I have to talk to him. "Please call me. I'm sorry."

I pick up my pace. I just want to be home. I run up the stairs to my room and promptly cry myself to sleep.

I wake when my phone buzzes again in my hand. I jump when I glance at the screen and see his name.

"I'm so sorry."

"You said that on your message."

"I mean it."

"I don't know what I did."

"You didn't do anything. It was my fault. I made a huge error in judgment, and I was just wrong."

He's quiet on the other end. "Thanks for calling me back," I say. "I was worried you wouldn't talk to me again."

"Funny, I was thinking the same thing."

I hesitate. "I told one of my friends about the experiment. She told Mrs. Carter. I thought it was you."

"Me? But I'm helping you with it."

"I know, and I can't explain why I didn't think it was her. It's just that she and I have been friends for so long. I never thought she'd do that."

"But you thought I would."

I go quiet. "I was listening to the wrong voices in my head."

"Be careful telling people about voices in your head," he says. Then I hear him laugh. "Get it?"

I shake my head. "You goof."

"I aim to humor."

"You do more than that. You're a good friend, Isaiah."

"You're telling me I missed school for nothing?"

My heart sinks again.

"I mean, I was going for the perfect attendance award and everything."

"I'm so sorry."

"You dork, I'm only kidding." He laughs at himself, and then adds, "So, other than that, how are things?"

"You mean other than being betrayed by my best friend and my dad failing to show up at the library yesterday? Fantastic."

"Andie, don't take this the wrong way . . . you know I'm all about helping you with this plan, but at some point, you promise me you'll get more help, right? Maybe this is bigger than what you're trying to do."

My muscles tense. Of course it is. I know that. I've always known that. But my dad doesn't even want me to go to the guidance counselor, so I don't know what else I can do.

"I need to give this a shot first."

"And if it doesn't work, then you'll talk to someone? I mean, someone who really knows something, not just Carter, who is a sorry excuse for a counselor." I hear the venom in his voice.

"What's your problem with her?"

"Nothing really. Just not a fan, that's all. You didn't answer my question."

"Come on, Isaiah, that's not all."

I hear him huff on the other end. "Fine. You know how I said Jeffrey made all that stuff up before, right?"

"Yeah."

"Well, sixth grade was rough. I used to go see her. She said I should apologize to him and that might make things better. Maybe Jeffrey was just embarrassed, she said."

"Oh no." I have a feeling I know where this is going. In real life it usually isn't as easy as just apologizing to a bully.

"Yup. Let's just say he didn't accept my apology and I never went back to Mrs. Carter." My feelings toward her and about her are getting more and more complicated. The Brian incident, the phone call to my dad, the way she acted today, and now this?

"I'm sorry."

"That's why I don't trust her, anyway. But there's got to be someone else who can help you," he says.

"I don't know for sure what I'll do if this doesn't work," I finally tell him. "I'll figure it out later."

Whether or not that answer is what he wants to hear, he doesn't ask me any more about it, and I'm relieved. I hear noises downstairs, and I get up and open my bedroom door.

My dad calls out, "Anyone home?"

"Hold on," I say to Isaiah, and then I call out, "I'm up here."

Dad steps out of the kitchen and looks up the steps. "Have you eaten?"

I shake my head and point to the phone. He nods. "There's food here when you're done."

I hang up quickly with Isaiah. I might not have a plan, but I don't want to miss a moment when my dad seems normal. I smell the pizza before I get halfway down the stairs and my stomach twists, telling me to hurry up, reminding me that I failed to eat lunch and was too angry to snack. It growls to the beat of food, food, food.

It's not just pizza, but there's also breadsticks and chicken wings. It's a feast. We haven't had a spread like this in ages.

"Hey, Candy. Hungry?" Dad's smile crawls all the way up to his eyes.

"Wow," I say, but I don't get anything else in because I've already grabbed a piece of pizza, picked a sausage off the top, and shoved it in my mouth.

"We're celebrating," he says.

I chew twice and swallow. "Huh?"

"I got a new job today."

My eyes go wide but my stomach does a flip, and I stuff more pizza in my face without asking him to elaborate.

He babbles as he gets a glass of water. The job is entry level and it doesn't pay quite as much as he'd like, but given the economy . . . he trails off, not mentioning any of the other reasons why he should be grateful for whatever job he can get. I want to be excited. I want to believe that this is it. We're going to be okay. But I've been down this road before. He's started jobs before, but then there are the bad days, then the long nights out; he's late a few times, and then he just stops going.

Before I decide how to reply, Paige walks through the garage door. "What smells so—" She stops mid-sentence, examines the room, and says, "Whoa."

Like me, she doesn't take much time to process the situation before attacking the food. The only pizza I've had recently was the two-dollar frozen kind. Definitely not like takeout.

I expect Dad to fill her in, but I glance at him and I realize he's nervous. Paige is a bigger threat than I am.

"Dad got a new job today," I tell her. *Please don't ask him how long it will last,* I beg her with my eyes.

I see the struggle on her face as she looks from me to him and back to me. "Oh? Where?" She stays calm and asks in a very matter-of-fact way, which must kill her, especially since I can feel the vibration of her shaking foot under the table. Her eyes squint slightly, but they're focused on her pizza. Maybe she's a little afraid of what his answer might be.

I study him for signs that he might be embarrassed to tell her. I remember his red cheeks when he told us he was going to sell cars. I also remember Paige's nasty tone when she yelled at him for not even being able to sell a used Toyota.

My Before daddy worked at a bank. He had a title I could never remember, but from what I could tell, it was a good job. That's why Mom stayed home. After Daddy didn't do well in jobs that had titles.

"It's at a bank, actually. I'll be a loan officer."

I don't know how that's similar or different from what he did before, but it doesn't sound bad to me. I bite my lip and lean in, wondering if Paige will feel the same.

"I didn't know you were looking to get back into the banking industry."

I almost giggle, because it sounds like something you'd hear old guys with bald heads and big bellies say. Not Paige with pizza sauce on her cheek and strands of hair falling loose from her ponytail all around her face.

"I wasn't sure what I was looking for, honestly. There hasn't been much out there in any industry, but it turns out an old colleague of mine now runs the loan department at this credit union. And he was . . . well . . . he just understood."

Paige nods. I smile. This is good.

"Anyway, I start Monday. I'll be there seven thirty to four thirty. Is that a conflict for anyone?"

I see Paige bite her lip, probably to keep from laughing since Dad's never here anyway. But we both shake our heads.

And then, for one whole hour, I don't think about my mom. I forget about Gisela and Mrs. Carter and my project with Isaiah.

I eat wings and choke when the sauce burns my throat. Paige tells stories about a bad customer, and Dad describes his interview in more detail.

I wonder if it will always be like this. In order to get a hint of regular, everyday life, I'll have to suffer through a whole lot of craptastic first.

Chapter Sixteen

I head back to my room around eight, planning to do home-work. I do have classes other than science, and I'm way behind in English reading and math worksheets. The prob-lem is that once I'm back in my room, my mom's journals call to me again. I haven't opened them at all today, and I miss hearing her words. I can afford to stay up late one night. I'll set a limit, I tell myself. Just one half hour. Maybe she'll help inspire me to figure out what to do next.

It can't be a coincidence that my dad has a job and we all sat down together to eat dinner for the first time in months less than a week after I started haunting them.

A half hour turns into two hours. This journal is mostly about my mom's frustration with Paige. She goes on and on for pages and pages about life with a teenager.

I called my mom last week. My mother managed to spend ten minutes telling me how everything I was doing was ineffective. I guess some things never change. She used to say the same thing about my study habits and my college major.

The one good thing about her criticism is that it took me right back. In the blink of an eye, I was a teenager again, listening to her constant barrage of complaints. No wonder I hated her then.

I thought about every conversation Paige and I had in the last week, and—surprise!—I'd spent most of the time trying to tell her what to do, how to think, and which clothes to wear. No wonder she's starting to hate me. New goal: bite my tongue more. Not on the big stuff—drinking, drugs, sex, etc. But it won't kill me to let her put blue streaks in her hair.

The streaks were ugly. In a rare moment of weakness, Paige even confided in me that she regretted getting them done, but she'd never have told Mom that. I wonder if that's the kind of thing that eats at Paige. The things you wish you would have said or the ones you wish you hadn't.

I've got a few.

Like, "Mom, I really was the one who broke your pearl necklace. I know you always suspected, but I was too scared to be honest about it."

Or, "I didn't really mean to say you were the most embarrassing mother in the room."

Wherever you go after you leave this world, I wonder if you still remember all that. Would it be better if you did or didn't?

It's late, but suddenly I have to hear her voice. Not just her words, but her actual voice. There must be videos somewhere. I tiptoe down the stairs. The living room is dark, but I don't turn on a light, not wanting to attract any attention. I open the cabinets under the television and rifle through boxes. Mostly, I find old DVDs from when Paige and I were young, like Disney cartoons and stuff. There are some unlabeled silver discs, and I keep them in a pile next to me. I figure I'll test them out on my computer.

I remember the video camera used to be in the cabinet in the sunroom/office. My mom picked the sunroom at the back of the house for an office because she didn't want to be far from everyone and stuck in the dark basement. So my parents put in a space heater for the winter and a window air conditioning unit for the summer.

Five big windows line the long exterior wall of the sunroom, and tonight the light of an almost full moon streams in. I haven't been out here in a while. Maybe no one has. The dust on the desk is deep enough to write a name in it. I doubt anyone has bothered to open a window or run the AC in months. Paige and I both have computers in our rooms now, and Dad, well, he hasn't been around enough to need it.

I open the cabinet, which is overstuffed with office supplies and general junk. Some people have a drawer. We have a whole cabinet. Batteries and Scotch tape, sheets of paper, and a box of miscellaneous electronics chargers. I don't see the video camera, but I spot the bag for her digital camera right away. It's got yellow daisies all over it. My mom wanted a fancy one, so Paige and I insisted Dad buy it for her for Mother's Day one year. That was the year she decided she was going to be a photographer. She carried the camera with her everywhere. We couldn't escape the lens. She insisted we not pose and would yell at us if we so much as smiled at the camera. She said the best shots weren't staged, and she was practicing finding the right aperture. Whatever that means.

I hit the power button, but it's dead—of course—so I dig through the bag for a charger and then drag everything to the office computer to plug it in so I can see the pictures on a bigger screen. I scroll through the most recent pictures on the camera, but all that does is make me sad. None of them are of my mom, since she was the one behind the camera. I need to see her face; I'm afraid I've forgotten details.

Apparently, no one has taken a picture on this camera since she died. I know it shouldn't surprise me, but it does. For a second, it's like life is frozen in the Before. Where Becki, Gisela, Leah, and I run through a sprinkler and squeal as we go down the slip and slide. Where Paige lounges in a bikini but sticks her tongue out at the camera when she catches it shooting her.

Even though she's not in the picture, I can see my mom smiling. I wish I could hear her laughter. I go back to the cabinet and look again for the video camera. I find the bag stuffed in the back. It's plain gray.

Unlike the digital camera, the video camera still has some charge in it and turns on right away. I press play, and it's a gold mine. The screen fills with her face. Her eyes are droopier than I remember. She has a few more lines around them, too. I sit cross-legged on the floor by the closet, staring that the tiny screen.

"It's May fifteenth and time for the end-of-year choir concert for Andie." She smiles bigger and the crinkles around her eyes grow deeper. "Another day, another school activity."

That's the last of her talking, as she turns the camera around and zooms in on my face. My mouth opens wide, and I join the choir in hitting a note so bad I imagine birds anywhere near the building fell from the sky. I press the red button to stop the video. I realize I've been playing it louder than I meant to.

I didn't hear anyone come into the room, but as soon as it's quiet, I hear the shuffling of feet, and then his shadow covers my face, making the office as pitch dark as the living room.

"What are you doing?" he asks. I can't get a read on this tone. He doesn't seem angry, but could he be scared?

"I wanted to hear her voice. I was looking for some video."

His face is a blur, so I have no idea how he registers what I've said. But I see him nod his head slightly. "There isn't much."

"I know." I hold up the camera. "This is from a long time ago."

I hear him sigh. Then it's quiet, so still even the air doesn't move.

Finally, he steps toward me, and I don't know what he's planning to do as he walks behind me and approaches the desk. As he starts clicking the mouse, I get up and head toward him.

"She downloaded most of them here. She's not in many of them, but sometimes you can hear her voice. They're all in the folder titled 'Video.' Think you can find it?"

I croak out a yes as he starts to walk away. I don't want to let him go. I feel like this is one of those moments that are likely to take him in the wrong direction. Instead of getting a message, he'll feel cruddy again. I can't have that, not with the new job and everything.

"Dad?"

"Hmm?"

"Have you watched them?"

"Yeah."

"I take it they didn't help?"

He exhales slowly. "It's a double-edged sword, Andie. You want to hear her. I know what that's like. But then you do, and you miss her fresh all over."

"Do you think I shouldn't watch?"

"Oh, Candy, I think you should watch your mom over and over if you want."

"Will you watch with me? Maybe it won't hurt so much if we do it together."

Please tell me I'm doing the right thing, Mom. If this is a mistake and it ruins everything, I'll have to give up on all of my attempts. I couldn't handle another bad reaction right now.

Dad doesn't answer in words, but he does sit down on the chair in front of the computer. He pulls up the folder he mentioned. I lean over the side of the desk.

"You pick," he says.

I bite my lip and scan the dates. I have to be strategic. I decide to avoid the most recent ones, because they're too real, too close, too much. Instead, I think about the journals, and I'm curious, so I point to a file with a date that lines up closest with the first journal entries I read. Me as a toddler. It's bound to be funny, and Mom is not likely to be at her best.

In the video, Mom is trying to get me to say all the words I know. "At nearly eighteen months, Andie now has sixty-two words." Of course, my mom counted things that weren't actually words, like "Whoo!" and words I say almost correctly, like "Ca" for cat. She gets frustrated when I refuse to show off my impressive vocabulary after only sixteen words. She tries offering me a snack as a reward, but I shake my head and say "No." In the background, you can hear my dad say, "I guess that's number seventeen." My mom busts out laughing.

But mostly the videos are short, and there aren't many.

"We got lazy about the video with you. Sorry, Candy."

"It's okay."

Finally we find a good one. It's my first birthday party, and Paige actually has the camera. I would have known even if she hadn't provided a running narration all throughout, because the camera is particularly shaky.

The good news is that because Paige is the one behind the camera, this time there are lots of shots of my mom, smiling and clapping and cutting cake and licking her fingers and carrying me around. I keep looking over at Dad, and he seems to be handling it okay. His eyes are fixed on the screen, but his shoulders are relaxed.

"Your mom hated that dress you're wearing, but Grandma Wilson had sent it, and she felt obligated to take lots of pictures of you in it."

"Grandma Wilson forgot my birthday this year."

He nods. "She always forgot unless your mom reminded her a few times." He leans back in the chair. "Your mom did so much that I never think about."

A thought explodes in my head. "You know you don't have to be her, don't you?"

His head tilts to the side.

"You can just be you, and that's okay." And I can't help myself, I crawl onto his lap and fall into his chest and I feel my tears dampen his pajamas. He wraps his arms around me and kisses my head.

"You're growing up too fast, Andie Candy. Too smart and too fast. I don't know what I'd do without you."

"Thanks, Dad." I sit up and sniff while I wipe the tears from my face. "I like hearing her voice again."

My dad stares at the paused screen in front of him. My mom is making a goofy face, trying to get me to eat some of the

Cookie Monster cake in front of me. I wonder if this will help or make things worse for him.

I tell him I'm tired and slink back upstairs. I reach down under my bed and pull out that journal, the one I already read about me turning one. Now it's time to do something for Paige.

I haven't heard him come up the stairs yet, so I quietly make my way down the hall. Opening Paige's door slowly, I can see her mouth is open and her arm is draped awkwardly over the side of the bed. She's out. So I sidle in and place the journal on her desk. In plain sight.

Chapter Seventeen

Watching the home movies with Dad may have been the right move, because the next morning he's sipping coffee at the breakfast table.

"You're up," I say.

He smiles. "I've got a meeting, and then I thought I should get this house in order before I start back to work. That office was looking pretty dusty."

"That's . . . good," I tell him. I don't mean to hesitate so much, but it seems *too* good to be true. I grab a Pop-Tart and lean against the counter. He glances down at his lap and then rubs his hands on his thighs.

"Well, I'm running late."

As he stands and carries his cup to the sink, I see his fingers shaking slightly. I say, "Good luck at your meeting."

"Thanks, Candy. It's not about luck, though."

And then I realize what kind of meeting he's talking about. I'm not stupid; I've heard of AA. We talked about addictions in health class, and I know there are meetings for issues other than alcohol—like gambling . . . I just never really thought of my dad as meeting material. But, of course, he is.

Once he leaves, I realize this is perfect timing for the next phase of my plan. I've decided to speed things up. Everything is happening quickly, and I don't want to miss an opportunity. And the sunroom is the perfect place for another direct message. It'll tie in with the movies from last night, and he'll see the sign when he goes in to dust later. I can hear water running upstairs, which means Paige is in the shower, so I go straight to the office and use my fingers to write in the dust on the desk. Just one word.

Whoosh.

It was dark last night, so Dad won't necessarily know when the word appeared. *Whoosh.* All my life it was something my parents said to each other, and I never knew what it meant. They said it was an inside joke. No matter how hard Paige and I begged them to let us in on the punch line, they never did.

But in the last journal I read, my mom told the story. It wasn't so much a joke as it was a way of saying *I love you.* Mom and Dad met at college. The sociologist and the business major. They were debate partners in speech class. She was not impressed with him. He thought she was flighty. They had to spend two weeks together, prepping for their first debate.

My mom wrote that he annoyed her the entire first week of preparation. He was so uptight and his views on the topic of whether or not the United States government "should significantly increase space exploration beyond Earth's mesosphere" were just as rigid. My mom, being the dreamer, was all for expansion. Apparently Dad was all about the dollars.

We could barely focus when we met, because we fought over the issue itself. I couldn't imagine how we would come together to defend the same position in such a short period of time. The hate was a thick fog, clouding my vision. It lifted on the eighth day. I'd begged him to let us work outside, as it was one of those gorgeous October Indian summer afternoons. I knew we'd only have a few warm days left. He'd grumbled about it not being very efficient, but for whatever reason, he relented.

We worked quietly for a while. I admit, I kept stealing glances at him. How had I not noticed how unique his eyes were? That rare shade of brown was such a nice complement to his olive skin. And that chin. Not quite square, but solid.

Then, a gust of wind came. Whoosh. Papers scattered. We scrambled to pick up all of our notes. He shrieked, and I laughed as I chased the papers. He said it was the image of me laughing and reaching for the papers that did it. He said the wind stirred up more than our homework. Whoosh.

I turned around once I'd caught most of the papers. A few were a lost cause. I shrugged and smiled.

His grin was bigger than I'd ever seen it. "You know, you're really pretty."

Whoosh went my stomach.

So, it stuck. From the beginning, it's what he would say to me whenever he wanted to let me know he loved me but didn't want to say the words. Just, whoosh.

I hoped he would see the word before he wiped it away with a duster.

Paige came out of her room in a daze. She barely said a word in the car ride to school. About a block away, she spoke without even glancing at me. "Andie?"

"Yeah?"

"Were you in my room this morning?"

I don't want to lie. I tried a trick I had actually learned from my mom. "Why?"

"Just wondering. So, were you?"

"Paige, why would I go in your room? I'm well aware that you would kill me if I stepped more than my toe in."

She laughs, but it's an absent sound, like she's not really in the car with me. It's okay. I know where she is.

As I get out of the car, she finally turns to me. "Can you walk home? I think I might go run after school today."

"Really?"

"Yeah. It's too late to join the team, but I bet the coach will let me tag along for some training."

I smile at her. "Have fun."

I'd almost forgotten about my own issues at school, but when I turn around I see my "friends" huddled not far from the car. Were they waiting for me?

I choose to look away and walk a straight line toward the building. I hear their feet behind me.

"You've got to listen to us," Becki calls out. "You're not being fair."

Her voice churns my stomach. "Fair?"

"The things you said last night. It's not that we can't talk about what's going on with you, but you've got to realize we still want to have a normal life, you know?"

I actually laugh. How could I not? It sounds so crazy. I turn around to face her. "Yeah, I know exactly what you mean. The problem, Becki, is that my life will never be normal again. Not the normal I knew before. And you know what? Neither will yours. Acting like you know everything and being mean won't bring your parents back together."

I know I'm being a jerk and I don't care. She deserves it.

"Oh my gosh, Andie," Becki says. "My parents have nothing to do with this."

"Yes, they do. You just haven't figured it out. You've changed too, and it's not fun anymore."

"Um, hello, I could say the same thing about you."

"Yeah, I'm sure you could. It's amazing how things like death and divorce can change you. I know I'm different. But I like to think I'm still me. I don't know who you are anymore."

Leah stares at her feet. She's never been good with conflict. She's always the friend who smoothes things over. She must know this isn't going to be so easy to fix. Or maybe she won't care enough to try this time.

Gisela is as red as a cherry. "Would you two just stop?" And then she marches off. Leah follows.

I'm not surprised. I stare at Becki, waiting to see how she reacts. "Are you happy now?"

"No, but neither are you."

"Is it a contest? To see who can be more miserable?" I snort. This is just like a Transitions session. "If it is, you can win if you want. I'm trying to find my happy again."

She rolls her eyes. "You sound like a greeting card."

Or a guidance counselor, I think.

"Anyway, maybe you should spend some time with your *new* friend instead of us. Maybe he'll make you happier."

I won't lie—it hurts. I'm too young to have been dumped by a boy, but this definitely feels a lot like a breakup. My lip quivers, and I have to ball my fists to keep my hands from shaking.

"Okay," I say.

"Have fun with your geektastic boyfriend."

The shaking stops instantly, and I turn on my heel and walk into the school.

I'm able to lie low most of the day. Except of course, I have group. I almost don't go, but I figure if I've ever needed therapy, today's the day.

I try to hide behind Amanda—the anger management girl—but she turns around and growls at me, so I get up and move. Since the two rows of seats are in a semicircle and all of the other back seats have been taken, I have no choice but to be visible. Only two open seats remain. One is next to Brian, which I refuse to take, and that means I end up sandwiched between a girl who probably hasn't eaten in two days and Dylan. He pats at the desk, knowing I'll choose that one.

Mrs. Carter breezes in just before the bell rings. "It's so good to see so many of you here today. With the end of the year coming, I worry a little about how everyone is going to be coping during the summer, so I'm glad you're checking in now."

Her chipper tone is a mask. She rustles her papers too many times for it not to be obvious that she's nervous. What's bugging her?

And then she clears her throat and sighs. "So, last week was pretty rough. I think we should talk about it."

Brian sits as straight as a steel rod, staring at the wall in front of him. "Andie should apologize."

"For what?" Dylan asks.

I try to sneak a peek at Dylan out of the corner of my eye. He's got his arms crossed as he smirks. "She didn't say anything that wasn't true."

Brian sits up taller. "She said my problems didn't matter."

"No she didn't," Amanda's voice is matter-of-fact, but it's so surprising to hear her defend me that I can't help but turn at look at her with my mouth open wide. "She said your problems aren't the only ones that matter. Big difference."

Mrs. Carter shuffles her papers and taps her pencil. "Well, Andie, do you have anything you'd like to add?"

I want to say no. I want to keep my head down and pretend none of this is happening. But Amanda and Dylan eye me expectantly. For the sake of everyone in this room, I probably need to talk.

"I had a really bad day last week. Really bad. And I've had some bad hours in between. But it's not all bad. In fact, I've been more hopeful than I had been in a long time. So, yeah, I lost it, and I get that I hurt your feelings, Brian. I'm sorry I yelled. But Amanda's right; I really do think we've all got something that sucks. It's just that if all we ever do is sit here and complain about it, it's not like it's going to get any better."

"Oh great, now she's Little Miss Sunshine," Amanda says.

Dylan laughs but his eyes narrow. "So, wise little one, what do you suggest?"

"I-I don't know exactly. I guess it just depends. Like, I've been trying to remind my family what my mom would have wanted and maybe it reminds them about who they used to be. Who they should be. It's probably stupid, but it makes me feel better, and my dad and I watched videos of her and he got a job, so it can't be all bad. But I can't say what would work for you because you've got different issues."

"Like psychosis," Amanda barks.

One side of Dylan's mouth curves up, and he nods slowly.

"Dylan,"—Mrs. Carter must have decided she should take the floor back from the thirteen-year-old—"what would you say your biggest problem is?"

"Duh, having to sit with all these freaks every week."

And there's the Dylan I know and don't love. Things were getting too real for a second, and anyway I'm just happy the attention is off me for a while. Brian is still pouting. We're so different—I guess we were never going to be best friends. But maybe group therapy doesn't always have to be so bad. Today was actually okay.

Chapter Eighteen

I figure there's no way I'll attend rec night now that Becki and I aren't talking, which is too bad because rec night is really fun. It'll just be another Friday night home alone. Now that I know where to find videos and I have the journals, too, I don't mind as much. After all, I've lost the last two days to late nights reading and rereading the same journal over and over. I'm so tired during the day that I have to fight to stay awake in class, and I don't do any more haunting at home. That probably doesn't fit in my whole do-something attitude that I preached to the group yesterday, but change takes time, right?

Then a couple of things happen to change my plans. At this point I feel just like I'm in a snow globe most of the time. Whenever things finally calm down, someone comes along and shakes everything up again.

I get home later than usual Thursday night, because Isaiah and I meet at the library after school to work on our report. This time, we didn't even mention my family or my side project. The actual science project is due soon, so believe it or not, we focus on the real assignment.

Just as I start walking up the driveway, I see the garage door open, and I hop on the grass as my sister backs out of the driveway full speed, then guns it once she gets to the street, not even bothering to wave at me.

"Dad?" I call out as I step into the house.

His voice cracks as he answers. "In here."

He's on the couch, in her spot. His eyes are a little red but he smiles at me. "Hey, Candy, how was your day?"

"Fine. Is everything okay?"

He takes a breath and his face contorts through at least three different expressions, but I can't figure out what he's thinking.

He pats the couch next to him, and I sit down.

"Paige is upset."

"About what?"

He raises an eyebrow.

I snort. "I guess I mean about what today? Besides the usual."

"Well, me, for one. She's not quite ready to open up with me, and I get it. Believe me, I do. I messed up pretty bad, and she doesn't trust me."

This is the first time he's admitted how bad he's been. I don't know what to say.

"I don't expect either of you to trust me yet. I don't even trust myself. Dealing with teenage girls, though, it's not really my thing. I wish I were better at this stuff."

"You know, Mom wasn't really all that good about dealing with Paige either."

His eyes narrow and his lips press into a line.

"I'm just saying maybe that's more about the teenager thing than Mom not being here."

He draws a long, slow breath, and then lets it out quickly. "Do you ever feel like Mom is trying talk to you?"

I raise one eyebrow.

"For a long time, I hated coming into this house because I couldn't feel her anymore, you know?"

I do, and I nod to show it.

"But it's been different lately. Not easier, but different."

"I like it when I smell her. Even when I know it's not her, it makes me feel like she's giving me a hug. I hope I never forget what she feels like."

"Me too, Candy. Me too."

He stares past me absently for a minute before looking back at me and asking, "How has Paige been dealing with her grief? Do you know? I know you meet with the folks at school, but I don't know how she's doing."

"I don't think she has."

"That's what I was afraid of."

"But she said she was going to go running today. I thought that was a good thing."

He nods. Then he grabs my hand.

"I wasn't sure whether to tell you this or not, but, um . . . your mother, she kept some journals. Paige wasn't interested in reading them, but you might be."

My mouth drops open and my heart skips a beat. That's what the fight was about.

I stammer out some sort of answer that involves thanking him and telling him maybe but not right now. *At least not until I can get them back into the storage tub,* I think. I hope I don't sound too crazy as I back out of the room saying something about being really tired now.

I have to get them back down there. I never should have taken all the diaries in the first place. I'd have been better off just taking one at a time.

What's weird is that Dad said Paige wasn't interested. I don't get that. Why wouldn't she be? Did she even bother to look at the journal on her desk? Did she read the words?

When I go to bed that night, I set my alarm super early, and at three in the morning I sneak downstairs and put them away. The whole time my heart races and my hands shake. But I don't get caught.

When I get up again at my regular time and make my rounds to wake everyone else up, I realize I had no reason to be nervous. No one was even home last night.

Chapter Nineteen

Dad had *just* told me even he didn't trust himself. I should have seen this coming. I don't know why I bothered to get my hopes up in the first place. I'm madder than ever. But not just at him this time. In fact, I'm probably less angry with him than I am at Paige. At least he's been known to mess up before. But not my Paige. Not my rock. She stayed out all night and didn't even come home for breakfast. I have to walk to school.

I wonder if I should tell someone. I'm really worried about both of them, but I know it will raise too many questions and open up all kinds of problems if I do. As I walk to school, I make a list of all the things that could have happened to Paige. I can't come up with any good ones.

Thankfully, she texts me right before I get to school. "Sorry, Andie. Overslept at a friend's house."

I don't accept the apology, but I'm relieved to find out she didn't end up doing something really stupid. I send a quick "OK" back to her. It's short and vague enough that she'll know I'm mad.

I feel a hand slap me on the back. "So, I've been thinking . . ." The gruff voice catches me off guard and I cough from the slap. "We should go to rec night tonight. Bring your little geek friend, too."

Amanda towers above me. Her arms are crossed and she looks so sure of herself, but I can sense the uncertainty in her voice.

"Why?"

"Aren't rec nights supposed to be fun?" *They are*, I think. *I love them.* With my friends, that is.

I shrug.

"Well, this is the last one of the year, and I've never gone. Something tells me Isaiah hasn't either."

"How do you—"

"I pay attention to things. And I've noticed you haven't been hanging out as much with your usual group, but you spend a lot of time with that kid in the library. Not my business, but I think you're better off. That blond cheerleader friend of yours thinks she's something special. I've heard some things she's said, too, and . . ."

"What things?" Becki may be mad at me, but the idea that she'd talk about me stings.

"She tells people you're crazy."

"What?"

"She laughs about the fact that you're in therapy."

"How do you even know that? You don't really hang out with Becki."

"I told you—I pay attention."

Maybe I've noticed Becki being meaner lately, and I know she can be thoughtless, but this seems extreme even for her. I don't know whether I don't believe Amanda or I just don't *want* to believe her, but I'm not ready to make nice.

"Why are you telling me this?"

"I'd want to know."

Don't shoot the messenger, I tell myself. She's right. I do want to know. But it's the last thing I want to know, too.

"But you're not nice to me."

"Andie, I'm not nice to anyone. You're not special."

That's true. I guess I can't say Amanda isn't honest. I wish I could say the same thing about Becki.

"So are we on? Rec night?"

"I don't know." I kick at a rock on the ground. "I'm just not sure."

She hands me a slip of paper with a phone number on it. "Let me know."

For the first time, when I look at her I don't see the angry girl who hits people and calls them names. There's actually only one case of her hitting someone, but now she's a legend, so people think it's more. That kid deserved it, though, because everyone knew he was tripping sixth graders and stuffing them in lockers. He just hadn't been caught yet. One day, Amanda just punched him as she walked past him at his locker. Didn't turn around or anything. After that, she just hit lockers next to people, enough to scare the pants off them. But right now, I only see a little girl who was always teased for being big. I think of Isaiah, who is always being made fun of for stupid stuff like being into science. "Okay," I say.

Later at lunch, I think maybe Amanda's idea isn't so bad. I eat my sandwich outside the library, and then Isaiah and I discuss strategy. This time we're talking about my home project again.

"I want to try something new."

Isaiah's eyes snap up from the page.

"I want to be even more direct. How about a recording?"

"Huh?"

"Can we splice words from video to put together a message?"

"Seriously, Andie?"

I nod.

His eyes are double their usual size and he scratches his head. "I don't know. How would it work?"

"I don't know. There are a bunch of videos on my mom's computer. I know I've seen things on TV where ghosts could make messages. There are all those YouTube videos where they do it."

"We could research it."

I sit up taller. I'm so excited that the tingles make my skin feel electric.

"How would you play it for them?"

That I had figured out. "Wireless speakers hidden in a room. It wouldn't be that hard."

"What if they catch you? This was not in the original plan."

"I know."

"Maybe you can do more with the smells thing," he says.

I've already blown that based on my conversation with my dad last night. Smells are out. I shake my head. "Nope. I need something new."

He begins clicking away on the computer, trying to find information about splicing. While he punches at the keyboard, I spring the next thing on him.

"We should go to rec night tonight."

He stops mid-click, but he doesn't speak. He goes back to typing. "It's not my thing."

"It would be if you gave it a try."

He laughs. "You make it sound like I should have just shown up at rec night by myself and had a great time."

My shoulders slump. "That's not what I meant. I just think we could have fun."

He turns away from the computer screen and faces me. His glare burns a hole right through me.

"Andie, I love hanging out with you, but I need to know, when your fight with your other friends is over, what will that mean for me?"

I grip the sides of the chair. "I don't think this fight is going to end."

He sighs. "But what if it does?"

Just tell him what he wants to hear, Andie. Don't leave him hanging. But I can't. I am so mad at Becki, but my friends have been my friends for so long that I can't promise they won't ever be more important again.

"Don't be silly," I say. "Just come to rec night with me."

He rolls his eyes, and looks back at the screen. "Maybe," he says.

But his maybe to me and my maybe to Amanda both turn into yeses by the end of the day. I had to say yes after I saw Jena Jordan standing in the circle with my friends between classes. It was like I'd been replaced already. Not that I have anything against Jena. She's just not me. Gisela sees me, and she waves. I guess you could call it a wave. She lifts her hand slowly and cautiously in my direction, anyway. I can't help but notice that she doesn't seem happy, but she also doesn't do anything to indicate that she'd like to talk to me.

At first, it's like a bee sting. It hurts, but I'll get over it, I think. But then, maybe it's more like a bunch of mosquito bites. Like when you get bit by a bunch of them at once and you have to suffer through the agony of a constant itch and annoyance. And the more you scratch, the more it hurts.

That's how I spent my morning—itching and trying not to scratch at my wound. I sit through social studies telling myself it doesn't matter. *I can make new friends. Ignore it. Ignore them.* I repeat that over and over. But of course it's a lie that not scratching a mosquito bite makes it itch less. It's still there, begging to be scratched. By the time I'm in my history class, I'm digging my fingernails in at rapid speed.

How dare they? Seriously, why are Gisela and Leah siding with Becki? What has she done for them? And where is my sympathy, darn it? Yes, I'm playing the sympathy card. What kind of friends won't stick by me when I've lost my mom? I thought they'd be with me forever.

But I decide they aren't going to keep me from having fun. I am a girl on a fun mission. If anyone deserves some fun, it's me. I'll create a fun caravan populated by me, Isaiah, and—for whatever crazy reason—Amanda. I just hope we're enough fun that she won't start hitting people. I wouldn't even know how to punch someone.

By the time class gets out, I'm done asking Isaiah; when I run into him in the hall, I demand he join me for rec night, and I expect him to be ready to have fun.

"Uh, okay."

"You know what? Let's do it up. Let's have pizza before we go. Oh, and Amanda is joining us. You know her, right?"

"Uh-huh." It might be my imagination, but I think when he heard her name he might have flinched a little. Common reaction.

I raise my arms up in the air. "Woo-hoo. Party!"

"You're scaring me, Andie."

I stick my tongue out at him, and he laughs.

I swing by Amanda's locker next. "Isaiah and I are meeting at Pizza Ranch at five thirty. Want to join us?"

There's a flicker of something in her eyes, but she stays cool as she shrugs. "Not sure. I'll see how I feel."

"Sounds good. See you tonight."

Chapter Twenty

At first, I'm alone at Pizza Ranch, and I feel like a complete moron. I sip a Coke and try not to look desperate. It's not like I'm the only kid to have the brilliant idea of going for pizza before rec night, so plenty of groups gather. Some with parents, some alone. It's too busy for me to even be tucked back in a corner. Nope, I'm completely visible at a table in the middle of the room. Alone.

Finally, at 5:43, I see the pouf of Isaiah's hair bobbing along outside the window, just skimming the tops of the booths. I would know that hair anywhere. Of course, so would everyone else, and I hear a table of girls giggle and I see them point toward the window. I guess no one expects to see Isaiah here. Maybe I should have picked Mama Maria's instead. No one goes there. *No,* I tell myself, *you have no reason to be embar-*

rassed. Still, my body betrays me a little when he bounces in. I feel my cheeks get hot.

"Sorry, my mom was running late."

More giggling from the table next to me. I command my cheeks not to turn red. *Do not let Isaiah see that you are a sorry excuse for a friend.*

Of course, now is the time Amanda picks to saunter in. Despite my best intentions, my cheeks flame so hot I wonder if I might explode, but when she sits down at the table, she turns and glares at the girls sitting next to us.

No more giggling after that. My cheeks cool. Maybe it's not so bad hanging out with someone who's tough. Then I look at Isaiah, and I swear he's shrunk into his chair.

"Uh, hey, Amanda. Do you know Isaiah?"

She smirks. "Who doesn't?" She reaches over and tousles his hair. "Why'd you quit coming to group?"

My mouth drops open and Isaiah's eyes shift to the table. Isaiah used to go to group, too. Of course.

As I look at him, he shrinks farther into his seat.

"So," I say, changing the subject. "What do you want on your pizza?"

Despite the rocky beginning, things take a turn for the better pretty quickly. It turns out Amanda is funny. Who knew? She does impressions really well. Her Mrs. Carter is dead on.

"And, Amanda, please tell me, how did it feel when you punched Joey Bartlett's locker?"

"Why, it felt fantastic, thanks for asking."

I laugh so hard my Coke sprays out my nose.

Even Isaiah loosens up. He still flinches every time Amanda slaps him on the back, but at least the fear is gone from his eyes.

By the time we get to school, embarrassment is the furthest thing from my mind. I'm having so much fun, I forget to care that it's with people who everyone thinks are too weird to hang out with.

Leave it to Becki to ruin that mood.

I hear the snort and know who it is before I even see her. *Be brave,* I command myself. *You're having fun. Who cares what she thinks?* I take a deep breath, turn around, and wave.

I see Becki roll her eyes, but Leah waves back, at least until Becki grabs her hand and puts it down.

Isaiah leans over. "Do you want to join them?"

I shake my head.

"So what's up with that, anyway?" Amanda asks. I'm starting to realize I like how direct she is. I'm tired of everyone dancing around the important questions.

"I wish I knew," I say. "It came on pretty quick."

Or did it? I think back over the past year. "I mean, it's always been hard since my mom died. They never knew what to say, but since things with my family have got more complicated, it's been even worse."

"Huh," Amanda says.

"What?" I can tell there's something behind her huff.

"I was just thinking about how you laid into Brian. It's made me think a lot about people and what we see, you know? I really don't think he knows that he whines all the time."

"Oh my gosh, he really does," Isaiah chimes in. "I ate lunch with him for a while last spring, and I couldn't stand it anymore."

"What does that have to do with me and my friends?" I ask.

"I don't know if it does. Maybe you just see things differently than they do."

I'm not in the mood to think about any of that. I'm in the mood for fun. So I shrug, and I announce there will be no more serious talk all night.

The school has been set up in different sections. I know the route my friends usually take on rec nights, so I am prepared to go a completely different way all evening. We can still run the circuit. There are video games set up in the library, and chess in one of the classrooms. Isaiah has already indicated that he has to play at some point. Amanda and I groan, but of course we'll go. I've never actually been to that area of the school on rec night before. There are some sports games in the gym, but none of us plan to shoot a basketball tonight, so we all agree the gym is off limits. In addition to other games throughout the building, there are snacks and music in the cafeteria. No one ever dances, but people like to stand around in their groups and act like they are on the verge of dancing.

My friends will mostly spend time in the cafeteria, but they also like to visit the gym—because a lot of boys hang out there. And Gisela likes to play volleyball. Amanda insists we head to the video game room first, which works for me. I've never been a big fan, but I won't have to worry about my other friends being there. I'm not really planning to play, but Amanda seems hardcore. She's talking about her stats on games I've never heard of.

The library is packed. Who knew? It's even busier than the gym usually is, but it's filled with kids I don't usually hang out with. People clear a path when Amanda walks in. Isaiah nudges me with his elbow as if to say, *"How cool is that?"* And it is. My friends and I fare well in the social world of middle school, but it's amazing how Amanda commands a room. I know it's not because people like her but because they're afraid of her, which maybe isn't a good thing. Still, I admit, it's kind of fun to walk behind her and have people wonder what's going on.

I see the awe in Isaiah's face. He's so used to being bullied that I can't imagine what it feels like for him to know that no one would dare say a word to him tonight. Amanda holds out her hand and someone puts a controller in it. And she really is fantastic. I don't think they're letting her win either, because she announced before she started that if anyone held back she'd slap them.

Kind of a mixed message, I guess, but whatever. Isaiah and I hang back and watch. We clap whenever she wins. No one else dares cheer for or against her.

At least an hour must go by, but we're not really paying attention to time because it's actually a lot of fun watching Amanda. She comes alive with a controller in her hand;

it doesn't even matter what game she's playing. I think other people start to see it, too.

When I concentrate, I tend to get this very serious look on my face. People always ask me what's wrong. Amanda's the opposite. The harder the game, the happier she looks. She laughs at obstacles and practically dances when her opponent is actually good.

"Who knew she could smile so much?"

I shake my head. "It looks good on her, though."

Isaiah nods.

I feel a tap on my shoulder, and somehow, I know it can't be good. I ignore it at first, until the tapping becomes more persistent and I hear Becki's voice. "Andie."

I turn slowly. She's alone. Or, if the others are here, they're mixed in with the crowd and I can't see them.

Becki pushes her bangs back. "Can I talk to you?"

Chapter Twenty-One

I'd hoped to avoid seeing my friends at all tonight, and this is almost too much. My heart is punching my ribs, and I'm only able to whisper, "I guess."

"In the hall?"

I don't want to go. I know without a doubt this is about to ruin my night of fun. Isaiah has inched closer to me, and I face him to ask, "Do you mind?"

He shrugs in response. Shoot, if he'd said yes, it would have given me an excuse not to talk to her, but of course it has to be my decision, and talking to Becki is the right thing to do. It wouldn't be fair not to hear her out since we've been friends for so long.

As we weave our way through the other kids, Becki grimaces and avoids touching anyone. Even a small brush makes her jump.

Once we're in the hall, she exhales. "Whew. What a zoo."

"Sometimes zoos are fun," I say.

"So, what's up with you?" She crosses her arms, and I take a step back.

"With me?"

"You've been acting so weird lately, and now you're hanging out with *them*? What are you trying to prove?"

"I'm not trying to prove anything. I'm just trying to have fun."

I don't know where she's going with this. "Just come on, and we'll figure out whatever's going on."

"Why?"

"Why what?"

"I'm having fun here. Why should I come with you?"

"Whatever. Come or don't come. I don't care, but your *real* friends sent me to get you."

Ohhh, so all isn't fabulous in Becki's world. My friends do miss me, at least two out of three.

"Where are they?" I ask. I crane my neck, trying to see if Gisela or Leah might be hanging out nearby.

"Around. Listen, we just need to fix this and get back to normal."

Her eyes shift left and right. I wonder if she's afraid someone will spot her back here by the geeky gamers or whether she's just nervous about talking to me. A part of me really hopes it's the latter. I want her to sweat a little. I want it to be important enough to her that she's scared she'll do the wrong thing.

But I don't get to find out which one it is, because right then, of all people, Dylan slaps me on the back. "Trouble in paradise?"

"Go away," Becki commands. Dylan does not obey. He laughs.

"Andie doesn't mind me, do you, Andie?"

"We're having a private conversation," Becki says, crossing her arms.

"Yeah, I'm sure it's important. 'Oh, what shade of nail polish should I wear next?'"

"Andie, come on, we'll talk about this later. Let's just go find Gisela and Leah and get away from . . . here."

It's like she can turn her emotions on and off, but my anger is stuck on on. "Um, I came with Isaiah and Amanda."

She raises an eyebrow and grins crookedly. "Seriously?"

I nod.

"You're not coming?"

I'm too scared I'll cry if I speak so I shake my head.

Becki turns and throws a hand in the air, talking to herself as she walks away. "I can't even believe you. Have fun with your freak friends."

Dylan gives my shoulder a subtle squeeze, then slaps my back as he walks away. I hear a kid scream, and I shake my head. I wouldn't have expected it, but Dylan is growing on me.

I take a deep breath. I guess that went about as well and as badly as it could have.

Behind me, the video game room is roaring with chaos. It looks like the players have taken a break from the tournament.

Kids start to file out of the room, and I have to squeeze past them and even push a little to get through. I've never liked big crowds. Not since I was like six. We were at a parade, I think, and my mom was holding my hand, but I got sandwiched between a couple of people. The guy in front of me had a great big Santa Claus belly, and my face pressed against it while the person behind me kept moving forward. I couldn't breathe, and I tried to scream, but the sound was muffled and nobody could hear me. I flailed my arms, hoping someone would notice. It felt like I was stuck there for an hour, but I know it was probably more like thirty seconds before my mom took hold of my hand and yanked hard, pulling me out from the crowd. She didn't say anything as she held me close and carried me through all the people. I cried into her shoulder, and it was uncomfortable because I was too big to be carried, and she kept having to shift her weight. My face bumped up against her collarbone, and her hands dug into my back to keep me in place.

She finally set me down when we were about two blocks away from the parade's path. She immediately collapsed onto the grass and breathed hard into her hands. By then, I'd stopped crying, but I sat down on the grass next to her.

She looked over at me and sighed. "I miss strollers."

"Me too," I nodded.

"You have to stay closer to me in those kinds of crowds, Andie. For a second, I couldn't see you, and it scared me half to death."

"I got stuck. I tried to keep up."

She took a deep breath, and reached out to touch my cheek.

Now I'm probably too big to get stuck in a potbelly sandwich, but I still feel my heart start to pick up its pace. Sweat beads at the back of my neck. It's easy to spot Amanda, and not just because of her size. It's that a circle has formed around her. Lots of kids want to talk to her. I can't tell if she likes the attention or not. She's smiling and answering questions, but she shifts her weight from side to side. I figure I'll have a better chance of finding Isaiah with her, so I make my way toward the group, twisting this way and that, hoping to see Isaiah's hair poking out from a group of kids. When it finally does, my heart sinks.

While Amanda has gathered a crowd of admirers, Isaiah is no longer with her, and the group that surrounds him, practically hiding him from view, is not there to congratulate him. They push him around like a pinball bouncing off the sides of the machine.

I should have known better than to leave him alone. I try to catch Amanda's attention for backup. I jump up and wave, but I don't think she sees me. I don't blame her; I doubt I'd be looking out for us either if I were her. But I have to do something to help Isaiah. There's only one of me and about five of them, so I'm rightfully freaked out even before they even notice me getting close. How am I going to get them to stop?

It would be different if my friends were here. Becki, Gisela, and Leah could stop people mid-sentence just by walking into the room. But they aren't here, and really, it's not like Becki would stick up for Isaiah anyway. She'd probably be more likely to join in the shoving. *That's not fair,* I think. She's been mean about Isaiah, but we're not bullies. Are we?

"Hey," I call out, but no one is listening. I yell out, "Stop!" but someone just swats me away. I'm not used to feeling so small and powerless. I'm not as brave without my friends. I wonder if I should just get in the middle myself. Would they bang me around, too? Probably.

Then, suddenly, Isaiah's hand reaches out between two of the bullies, and I don't know whether he heard me and knew I was there or was just desperate. I don't care. I grab his arm with both my hands and yank as hard as I can. The kids surrounding him aren't expecting it, so when he breaks through between them, one stumbles off to the side and the other just stands there with his arms dangling at his sides.

"Not smart there, girlie," a girl dressed all in black says. "Your friends aren't here to back you up."

"What did you say about friends not being here?" Amanda towers above me. She's also at least a head taller than the girl in black standing in front of us.

"Right, like you two are friends." Goth girl folds her arms and huffs.

Amanda smiles. "It seems Andie has learned the value of diversification."

The other girl drops her hands and her eyebrows crinkle. "What?"

176

"Come on, kids, let's go get some punch."

Isaiah and I follow Amanda like ducklings. I might even waddle a little trying to keep up. She has super long legs and she's on a mission, so she doesn't turn around to talk to us at all.

Isaiah leans over to me. "Are you okay?"

I stare at him with my mouth hanging open. "Are you kidding?"

His face drops; he genuinely looks hurt. "No."

"You were just surrounded by a bunch of jerks, and you wonder how *I'm* doing? I'm fine. My talk with Becki was a walk in the park."

Amanda stops mid-stride. "You talked to her?"

"Yeah. I wish I could say she came to apologize."

Isaiah leans up against a locker, breathing hard. "I'm sorry. I think it's my fault."

I raise my hands in question. "What are you talking about?"

"I knew she didn't like me. It's not like I thought being friends with you would mean everyone would start being nice to me, but I didn't think they'd start being mean to you."

"It's not your fault, Isaiah. It's really been coming for a while. Anyway, I think my other friends are mad at her, and that's why she came to talk to me, not because she really wanted to make things better."

"You know"—Amanda runs a hand through her hair—"sometimes, it sucks not having friends, and then sometimes I think I'm the lucky one. If the people who are supposed to have your back treat you like that, then what's the point?"

Isaiah laughs. "Wow, I know exactly what you mean. I used to get really mad that I couldn't be popular, and then I started hanging out with Andie, and I've decided that I'd rather have good friends than popular ones."

It's kind of an insult. But I don't tell him that because I don't want to ruin the moment for either him or Amanda. Still, I wonder if we've always been seen this way by other people.

And is there hope now? Were we only friends when there were no problems? Was our friendship on such a tightrope that all it took was one fight to make us all fall off? Did wanting to be popular do that to Becki? I don't think it has to. I don't think of my friends that way, and I never did. I didn't think about popular or unpopular. I just thought about friends. Now, I don't know what to think.

"Why don't we head out for ice cream?" I suggest.

My mom taught me an awful lot, but Dad may have given me the most important knowledge on the face of the earth: ice cream fixes everything. On the really bad days, he'd heap a bowl with several scoops, some fudge and some whipped cream, and before you knew it you couldn't help but crack a smile. It never failed. I figure it can't hurt for us to try that, too.

Chapter Twenty-Two

After rec night, I decide it's time to step things up. If one night can make such a difference with my school life, what can I do in one night at home? I stay up late brainstorming, and before I crash, I take some notes so I won't forget. Then I flop down on my bed until my phone vibrates in my hand a few hours later. It takes me a while to register why as I sit up and fumble to turn off the alarm. It's three thirty; another too-early morning for me. I'm groggy as I wipe the crusties from the corners of my eyes. I lie back down. Maybe this is a bad idea.

I let my eyes close for just a moment, and I'm tempted to fall back to sleep. But in the dark, a movie plays out on the backs of my eyelids. I see my dad at the casino. I see my sister working at the diner.

She looks older. That's what makes me sit back up with my eyes wide open. *No,* I tell myself. *Something has to change.* Paige has to go to college. And she won't go unless my dad stays on track.

Isaiah and I didn't get very far with our splicing research, so I've decided to go back to smells after all, at least with Paige. I never did figure out a way to make bacon and hide all the traces, but Isaiah had the brilliant idea of using bacon dog treats instead—they're a lot easier and smell enough like the real thing. I pull one from my backpack and step into my sister's room. Her soft snoring tells me she's sleeping. She's got the covers pulled over her head with one foot sticking out at the bottom. Typical Paige. I like that. A lot of mornings when I wake her, it's pretty clear she's been all over the bed, not sound asleep like she is now. I walk on tiptoe, hoping she hasn't left anything on the floor. I know her room well enough that I should be able to get through in the dark, but a random shoe or a hairbrush could blow the whole thing.

I have one small incident when I misjudge the distance and run into the corner of her dresser. The sharp edge presses into my arm, and I have to clench my jaw shut to keep from making a sound. She doesn't even turn, so I exhale. I quietly make my way over to her bed and slide the fake bacon under her mattress. If she wonders about the smell, she might check under her pillow, but I don't think she'd bother to look further.

Next, I stumble into my dad's room. I've come up with something new for him. He's also sleeping soundly. I'm grateful for his loud snoring, which covers the shuffling of my footsteps on the hardwood floor. The bathroom door creaks when

I start to open it, and I hear him grumble and then turn over. I freeze outside the doorway. If he wakes up now, I'm caught, because the bathroom light is on, and it would be impossible for him not to see me standing here. I forgot about that. Mom always wanted the light. Dad teased her about being afraid of the dark. I wonder if he still leaves it on for her.

I wait for what seems like several minutes, not moving a muscle. My legs start to hurt. Finally, I turn and slip in sideways through the door. Not wanting to open it any farther, this is the only way I fit.

I carefully open the vanity drawers under the sink. As I expected, my mom's side is basically empty. All of the bottles of nail polish and the bazillion makeup brushes were tossed in the great purge several months ago. I dip my fingers into my pocket and feel for two items. First, I take a tube of lipstick in pale pink, the only color my mom ever wore, and I place it in an empty drawer. Then I open the drawer under it, where dad keeps his shaving stuff. Next to his navy blue razor and the bottle of shaving cream, I set a pink Venus razor. I've even used it a few times to make it look worn. I tuck it in at an angle, hoping it looks natural in there, as if it had just been hidden and rolled loose after all this time.

Then, I hoist myself up onto the counter. My feet dangle off the end and I lean in close to the mirror. I open my mouth wide and breathe on it. The "ha" that escapes echoes a little in the sparsely filled bathroom. I have to take another breath and do it again to cover a large enough area on the mirror. Once

I create a patch of about four inches by four inches of fog, I use the tip of my finger to write in long loopy letters. I don't write "whoosh" this time. I thought long and hard about what to write in this message. I didn't want it to be too big, so "I love you" was out. And since I've decided that I need to be more direct with my dad, I've settled on four letters:

L-I-V-E

I mean it as a command, and I hope he sees it that way. It's the simplest way to tell him what I think she'd want him to know. She's not here, but he is. I watch as the fog fades and my word disappears. I nod to myself. When my dad showers, the steam will cover over the mirror again, and with some luck my message will show up, just subtly enough that he won't be able to tell who or what did it.

I got this idea from the ghost literature I've been reading. Ghosts can't move much, but this is the kind of matter they might be able to influence if the energy is aligned right. You know, if you believe in that sort of thing.

I sneak back out of the room. Next, I go downstairs to the living room. We don't have an overhead light in the room, but there's a floor lamp that's connected to an outlet, so when you flip the main switch it comes on. It's one of the things my mom hated about this house—she always thought the living room was too dark. But it works in my favor now. I twist the bulb a bit, just enough so that it should flicker when anyone flips the switch. Hearing no noise upstairs, I test my theory. It's eerie. Perfect.

I duck into the garage and spray just a hint of my mom's perfume in my dad's car, on the passenger side. It's a risk, but I know I have to do something extra to make sure he puts all the pieces together.

It's still early. No one should be up for a while, but I have one more thing to do.

Chapter Twenty-Three

*P*aige will go off to college in less than two years, and that thought sometimes stops me in my tracks. Literally. I'll be in the kitchen making coffee and I'll just start crying. How can my baby graduate college? How can she be a grown-up? Who will I be when she's gone? And don't even get me started about how I'll handle it when Andie goes.

This is something they don't tell you when you have kids. Your identity becomes so wrapped up in them that you forget who you are, which is fine if your kids actually did what they were supposed to do and reflected well on you. I'm only half kidding here. If my identity is being a mom, then what happens if my kids fail? Does that mean I fail, too?

I know I'm supposed to let my kids be who they are and find their own paths in life, but I admit that I've looked for their strengths and tried to push them to hone those skills in positive *ways. So, now, I'm completely flummoxed when Paige says she doesn't know what she wants to major in. She's thinking business. Business? What do you mean business? I've been training you to be a lawyer your whole life. How did you miss that?*

Now, I'm more than half kidding. I don't really care what my kids do for their careers. Or if they have a career. I'd be a horrible hypocrite if did. After all, I don't have one.

College, however, that's a must, even if they major in basket weaving. I'm pretty sure if one of them didn't go to college, it's one of the few things that would make me feel like a true failure.

When I read those words, I knew that I had a new goal. That, beyond everything else, there was a real reason for me to do what I'm doing, and it didn't have to be that I just wanted my family back to normal. That's great and all, and, of course, that's what I want, but just wanting that has started to make me feel selfish. What a crazy, idiotic plan this has been if it's only for my selfish needs. But this—this is a real reason. My mom had a plan for us, and everything tells me Paige will blow that plan if changes aren't made.

In the basement, I trade out the current journal for one I had already tucked back in the tub. I don't leave before I lose almost another hour reading more of my mom's words.

I don't leave the basement empty-handed, though. I grab two items I'd noticed the last time I was down here. The first is my mom's phone. I know it won't have service anymore, but I was surprised when I saw it, because I thought it had been destroyed in the crash. It is a little banged up, a corner is dented, but Dad must have kept it for a reason.

I run my fingers over the buttons several times before I'm finally brave enough to press the green On button. Nothing happens, of course. I dig back into the tub and find the charger, then I scoot over by the wall so I can plug it in. I don't know what I expect to see. I assumed my dad had canceled service on it, but almost instantly, there's a *ding*. Eleven new voice mail messages. And forty-two new texts.

My heart lurches in my chest. They must be from people who don't know. I used to hate those awkward calls to the house or run-ins with acquaintances at the grocery store.

"How's your mom?"

"Dead."

I imagine that wouldn't go over too well, so instead usually there was this strange dance where I would shuffle my feet and look at the ground while stammering out something about an accident. I didn't like to see their faces when realization hit them. It was embarrassing and awful for both of us, and inevitably I would tear up at some point. It's hard to get past the shock of your mom being gone when you constantly have to tell people who are hearing it for the first time.

When I open up the voice mail, I can see there are probably a few of those—mostly from 1-800 numbers, so they're probably credit card companies or charities. I ignore them. My eyes are drawn to one number that takes over most of the history.

It's my dad's cell phone number. He calls her. Still.

He never stopped.

I can't listen. I shouldn't listen. I back out of voice mail and open the texts instead.

Other than a few from her service provider telling her about some deal, they're also all from him. The texts are short, like texts usually are. But I can see the story that's being told between the lines.

"Where do you keep the insurance files?"

"What kind of spaghetti sauce do you buy?"

"Missed you at lunch today."

"Won $100 on slots but lost $250 at poker."

"Paige quit track. I'm sorry."

"Went to a meeting today. Couldn't make it through."

It's like someone took cotton balls and stuffed them down my throat. I can't breathe. I shouldn't see this. It's too personal. My shaking hand goes back to the voice mail screen. *Just one,* I tell myself. It wouldn't be fair to listen to them all, but one can't hurt anything, can it?

I set the phone down. *No, I shouldn't. I won't.* I pick it back up. *But I can't not.*

I pick a random date. I figure it will be less obvious if he ever sees that they've been listened to.

At first, I barely recognize his voice. It's quiet, muffled. Then I hear the tears, and I feel like someone threw a brick at my stomach. It's not that I haven't seen my dad cry before. But even after Mom died, during the funeral, at the house, it was only silent tears. His eyes would be red, but he'd still stand there greeting people.

This is choked sobbing. His words come in starts and stops.

"... can't do it. What's wrong with me?—How could you do this to me?—Sometimes I hate you.... No, you know I don't."

I hang up. Not this one.

I press another date. This one's more recent.

"Hi. It's been a few months. I know you're not listening, but it feels good to pretend you can hear me. When I talk to the air, it doesn't feel the same. I've been thinking about you a lot lately. Not in the usual way. I miss you, of course, and I usually think about what you'd be doing if you were here and how much easier life would be. But lately it's been more about where you are. Where are you? Andie still reads those stupid ghost books, and I picked one up when I saw it lying there in her room the other day. Are you a ghost? Are you around us, still? Can you see us? Anyway, that's what I've been thinking about lately. I'll talk to you soon."

It takes me a while to catch my breath. I don't cry, but my lungs are frozen.

I wish I could talk to him about these things. It's not like I haven't thought about them. I wonder if Paige has too.

I wonder what would happen if I tried to tell my dad that I wonder the same thing. I don't listen to any more of the messages. It isn't that I don't want to. More than anything I want to know everything my dad's been going through and all the things he's been thinking. A big part of me thinks I have a right to know. I even consider taking the phone and showing it to Paige. She'd have a better idea what to do with these messages. But on the other hand, these messages are like my dad's diary. I wouldn't want him reading mine, if I had one, anyway. I only feel okay about reading my mom's journals because she's not here anymore.

So I drop the phone back in the box.

Chapter Twenty-Four

I've lost so much time that as soon as I get to the top of the steps, I get nervous. I can't believe I'm actually hoping this is one of my dad's bad days. I shut the door quietly behind me and I keep an ear out. It seems quiet. So I walk/run through the kitchen.

As soon as I turn the corner, I practically run straight into my dad.

"Why the race?" he asks as he rubs his eyes.

"I need to wake up Paige."

"Oh," he says.

"Did you just get up?"

He nods, clearly not entirely awake yet. I breeze past him, jog up the stairs, slip into my room to hide the journal I left sitting on my bed, and then go to Paige's room, where I knock several times and call out to her.

At first, I hear her groan, and then something must click. *Bacon*, I think. Because her voice sounds very clear when she calls out, "Did you make breakfast?"

"Uh, no," I say, using my best *duh* voice.

Then I sort of skip back to my room. So many traps lie around the house this morning. It's almost like a grand finale of a fireworks show, but I know it's not over yet. There's another big boom to come. I'm excited and nervous at the same time. And since listening to my mom's phone, a small pit of guilt has settled in my chest. If my dad is wishing she were a ghost, is it wrong to give him hope?

I tap my fingers on my dresser as I stare at my reflection. Should I stay or should I go? I could say I needed to take off early to meet up with Isaiah. Then I'd miss the chance to *ooh* and *aah* at the Fourth of July explosions, but I also wouldn't have to try to keep a straight face so I don't look guilty or deal with any potential backfire.

After taking a deep breath, I decide I need orange juice before I can decide, so I head back downstairs. Paige hasn't come out of her room yet. As I pass her doorway, I can hear her opening and closing drawers.

Downstairs, my dad sits in the living room, staring at the flickering lamp.

"What's up?" I ask, because it would be weird not to say anything.

"Broken lamp, I think."

"That's kind of weird, huh?"

He nods, but he doesn't break eye contact with the lamp.

I would leave—I *should* leave—but my dad's confused, pathetic expression holds me captive. "You need anything?" I ask him.

He shakes his head slowly. "I'm going to shower."

My fists clench as I watch him set his coffee mug down and exit the room. Now I *really* should leave, but Paige is standing in front of me, her expression unreadable. Just sort of blank, like my dad's.

She sees me and says, "I'm in the mood for breakfast. How about you?"

No, you should not stay for breakfast, I tell myself. *You're walking on a high wire.* "Sure" slips out of my mouth before I remember that I should be "leaving early to meet Isaiah." "I can start it if you want."

She smiles and says something about me being the best little sister ever, and then goes back upstairs to finish getting ready. My head is spinning.

In the kitchen, I check the dates on the eggs. They're still good, so I scramble up a bunch and throw some bread in the toaster. We don't have any bacon, and I'm glad. I'm not sure I could have made it through seeing anyone eat bacon.

That ten minutes or so is quiet—a calm before the storm. My eggs are pretty, fluffy and yellow. I even find strawberry jam in the cupboard for the toast. I set the table with actual forks and knives and real plates instead of paper ones. I fill a glass of juice for Paige and top off my dad's coffee. Then I wait. Dad might as well be a ghost himself when he returns. All the color has faded from his face, and he walks as if floating.

Paige slides into a chair and pokes at the eggs with her fork. I think Dad eats his just to be nice. Their thoughts must be heavy, because their heads both hang low over their plates. I hadn't planned what would come next when I did all this today. I knew eventually they would talk to each other about everything that had been happening, but I didn't expect it to start right then.

"I smelled bacon this morning." Paige speaks in a low, soft voice, still staring at her eggs. "Why does bacon remind me of Mom?"

I smile. "Bacon reminds me of Mom, too," I tell her.

Dad whispers, "She sure loved bacon." Then he pauses before adding, "I swear I smelled her perfume today."

Paige's head snaps up. "I've smelled her perfume, too. The other day on the couch."

"Really?" Dad leans toward her. "I've had other things, too. Like messages."

"Me too!" Paige sits up taller. "Not just the journal either. Wait, does Andie know about the journal?"

She's pointing at me, and Dad is nodding. "I told her."

"Anyway, I swear a picture was moved. What about you?"

"Words in dust. Words on my mirror. Her words." He sets his fork down. Paige looks at him, wide-eyed. "And the lamp this morning."

"What? You saw writing? From Mom?" Paige's voice has gone higher, and I'm afraid to look anyone in the eye, but I glance up, and I catch my dad's eyes narrowing.

"Calm down, Paige. I might have imagined things. I'm not sure what I saw."

Out of the corner of my eye, I see Paige's face crumple a little. "What about you, Andie? Have you seen anything odd?"

The wheels in my head spin. What I want to answer is that I've seen lots of odd things lately. That my dad gambling away insurance money and my sister giving up on college are odd enough for me without worrying about Mom's ghost. I want to tell them that the best messages I've had from Mom lately were her own. Her journal and the video of her. That's the point of all of this, after all. To remember the real mom, not the ghost mom. But I don't know how to say that right now when Paige is excited. I'm so scared of getting caught that my knees are shaking under the table.

I shrug a shoulder and take a bite of my eggs. I'm chewing as I say, "Don't think so."

Paige isn't giving up. "Do you think there's any way . . ."

Dad cuts her off. "No, Paige. This isn't one of Andie's books. Mom is gone."

"But there are so many coincidences. Isn't there a possibility?"

"You know ghosts aren't real."

"Andie thinks they're real, don't you? You're always reading about them."

"I don't know. Maybe." I put my fork down and shrug. "I . . . I'm actually doing a science project on it."

Dad raises an eyebrow. "Really? A science project?"

I sit up a little straighter. "Yeah, Isaiah and I have a semester science research project, and we decided to explore scientific theories of ghosts."

"The teacher was okay with that topic?" I can't quite read my dad's face, but I hear concern in his voice.

I nod.

His brow furrows, and I wonder if this is it. Is this where we get to finally really talk about things? About how we're feeling and about whether we think there is an afterlife?

"Seriously? The teacher let you do that?" Paige's mouth hangs open a bit. Then she cocks her head. "What have you figured out? Anything good?"

Dad shakes his head slightly and starts collecting plates. He makes a lot of noise, but I can feel his eyes on me. "Not now. You two better get going. I'll take care of cleanup. I'm sure this is all just coincidences."

"Too convenient," Paige says, as she pushes her chair away from the table. She smiles though. She's the one who seems most excited about the idea that Mom's ghost might actually be haunting us. Now that I know about Dad and the phone, I think maybe Paige is the one who's been hiding away all her emotions. Maybe while she held everything together, she's been the most lost.

As we ride to school, Paige peppers me with questions about ghosts. I explain all the theories I know. I've told her some of this before, but she's getting more serious with her questions. She starts bringing up other signs. Things I didn't do.

Like the time her car wouldn't start, but she said she wished Mom were there and then when she turned the key, the engine flared up.

Or the time she didn't have any money to put gas in her car, but she found a five-dollar bill in a purse Mom had borrowed just a couple of days before she died.

She lists enough things that even I start to wonder . . . is it possible? Could Mom really be around and somehow I didn't notice? Have I been missing real signs all this time I've been planting fake ones?

Paige is about to drop me off at my usual spot in front of the school, but I motion for her to go around to the back entrance.

"Huh? But your friends are right there. I can see Gisela standing by the doors."

"I just don't want to see anyone this morning."

"Did something happen?"

"Well, Mom died," I say. She whips her head toward me, but then she must see in my face that I'm serious. "That sort of changed everything," I add.

Paige runs her hand across the steering wheel and exhales. "Yeah. That it did."

"Anyway, it hasn't been fun, but I'll be okay." It's funny because, for the first time, I think I might actually believe that.

She reaches out for my hand and gives it a squeeze. "Let me know if you need to talk."

I need to talk every day, I think. *I've needed you to talk to me every day since Mom died*, I want to tell her.

"Thanks," I say instead. "You, too." And I mean it.

My morning is actually pretty normal, all things considered. I don't run into Becki or anyone else—I'm getting good at avoiding them in all their usual spots. Amanda high-fives me as she passes in the hall, and I swear some kids looked at me with awe after that. Hey, I'll take what I can get.

It isn't until I'm called out of class to Mrs. Carter's office that anything unusual happens. My heart immediately begins to jackhammer. The last time I was called out of any class, I learned about the accident. When I get to her office and see my dad sitting in the room, my first thought is *Paige*.

But his face isn't sad. For the first time in a long time, my dad looks mad, which kind of scares me. I wasn't sure it was even possible for him anymore. His emotions have been so absent. But his brow is crinkled and his lips are tight. He massages his temples, something he always used to do to keep from blowing up when he was mad.

For a split second, I consider making a run for it. Maybe they didn't notice me come in—I can sneak back out the door, get down the hall, and hide in the bathroom by the art hall or something. Whatever is going on, I just know this is not a conversation I want to have.

I take one step backward, but I'm too late.

"Andie," Mrs. Carter says, motioning to the chair next to my dad, "shut the door behind you and have a seat."

I don't bother to ask if everything is okay. I already know it's not. And I'd be lying if I said I didn't have a clue about what is going on. There is only one thing that could bring these two together today.

Chapter Twenty-Five

"Your dad called me today. He said he's been worried about you and he knew we had chatted some. I did not share anything from our sessions, just so you know."

"Okay," I croak out.

"I found this," my dad adds. He sets Isaiah's chart on her desk. "What are you trying to do, Andie?"

I remind myself to breathe in and out. How could I have been so stupid? When I don't say anything, Mrs. Carter joins in again.

"Andie, in the course of our conversation, your dad mentioned some things, and based on your friend's warning last week, I shared with him my concerns that you might be doing something to make your family think your mom's ghost is still around. Your father did some searching."

I appreciate her play-by-play and wanting to let me know what had actually happened and all, but at the same time I just want my dad to say something.

"How could you do that?" he asks. He won't look at me. "I can't believe you would do that."

"I had to do something," I argue. "You weren't." I don't know where that last part comes from, and I instantly feel guilty for saying it even if it's true. I don't want to get Dad in trouble with Mrs. Carter.

"That's not fair, Andie. You really have Paige hopeful that your mom is trying to contact us. Is this part of your project?"

I shake my head. "It's not like that."

"Then what is this?" He holds up the chart, the one Isaiah made. "Are you experimenting on us?"

Tears stream down my face. "No, you don't understand."

"Of course I don't understand, Andie! What were you thinking?"

"What was *I* thinking? What were *you* thinking?" Suddenly, I blow up, not afraid to burn anyone in the process. He opens his mouth to speak. His eyes have softened a bit, but I don't care now. "You're the one who checked out, not me. Do you think we don't know what's going on? The jobs? We're not stupid. You never talk about her. You never talk to us at all. And then you want to know what's up with me? You hid the journals and her rings and didn't tell me about the videos! And you call her! You call her! But it's like the rest of us can't even talk about her!"

I have to stop to take a breath. My chest heaves.

I see in my dad's face that he's stunned. I'm not sure he can speak. I don't know what else to say so I just let the whole admission hang out there.

Slowly, my eyes drift to Mrs. Carter. And I almost laugh. For as much as she begs for honesty in sessions, this might have been a little too real for her. She grips her pen so tightly, you'd think someone was trying to steal it from her. The muscles in her neck are clenched together, and her wide eyes don't blink.

She finally breaks the silence. "Well, it's good that you're both expressing your feelings. It's seems you've been holding back with each other."

My dad huffs. I have a feeling we're thinking the same thing.

"Perhaps it would be best for Andie to take the rest of the day off, and for your family to use the time to process everything you've learned. I have some phone numbers here. I can refer you to some professionals who are better equipped to help you heal."

Oh that's rich. She's going to pass the buck.

Mrs. Carter fumbles in her desk drawer for a piece of paper and holds it out for my dad. He eyes it but doesn't reach out at first. I don't know whether it's his skepticism about psychiatrists that's causing him to hold back or whether he, too, is afraid to be dismissed. What will we do once we leave this room? Then we'll have to talk to each other. For real. We've made strides in the past few days, but now that I've said every-thing out loud, we really have to face the truth. Mrs. Carter looks so uncomfortable, but her hand doesn't waver. I'm about to relieve her and grab the piece of paper myself when Dad finally takes it from her. He immediately folds it in half and then again before standing and stuffing it in his pocket.

"Do I need to stop at the office or anything?" Dad asks. "To take her home?"

"No, it'll be fine. I'll take care of it." She gives us both a tight-lipped smile. "Andie, will you step outside for a moment?"

My mouth goes dry. As afraid as I am of being alone with my dad, this might be worse. Are they going to talk about me? Is she going to suggest some sort of punishment? I stand slowly, and my knees feel shaky, but I walk toward the door.

"You can shut it on your way out," she says.

I glance at my dad, but he won't look at me, so I do as she requested. The school walls are old block concrete, painted bright yellow, and they're too thick for me to hear any details through. Muffled voices sound clipped but controlled. I tap my foot and lean against the door, desperately trying to hear what they're saying. I jump away when I see the doorknob start to turn and lean against the cold yellow wall.

Dad says nothing, but motions for me to follow him. I have to jog a few steps to keep up because he's going so fast. He must be really mad. I begin to imagine what kind of punish-ment he might come up with.

Dad's never really been the disciplinarian in our house. I guess we're not like most families. Leah's mom always used to warn her, "Just wait until your father gets home," and that would make Leah snap right into line. Becki's dad never had to do much of anything, but he was just so big that if he stood over you and stared, you wanted to behave instantly. And Gisela's dad is a softie, but he had a way of telling stories about how he was disciplined when he was growing up that made you not want to push any limits with him.

In my house, Mom is the one we fear. Or feared, I guess. Not that she was mean or spanked us or anything like that, but she could always figure out what punishment would be the worst. It was like she could hear our silent pleas. *Whatever you do, please don't tell me I please don't tell me I can't go on the water park trip.* Then, of course, that's the thing she'd take away. Dad yelled louder, but he didn't have a lot of bite behind the bark. When I was little, it made me run to my closet and cry, but as I got older, I could pretty much ignore it unless I thought it was going to lead to Mom stepping in with her brand of punishment, too.

I brace myself for yelling. I consider stuffing Kleenex in my ears, but then I remember I don't have my backpack. I'm too afraid to tell my dad. I don't think he'll care, and I'm probably not doing any homework tonight anyway.

He still doesn't say anything even when we're outside. Okay, he must be saving it for the car. But even after the doors are shut, and the AC is running, he doesn't say anything. I'm not sure what to do. Am I supposed to talk? Should I apologize? Will that make it worse? This is all fairly new territory for me. I've never been in big trouble before, not the kind where you get pulled out of school, and, even if I had, it would have been Mom coming to get me. She would have started talking the second we walked out of Mrs. Carter's office, telling me how disappointed she was in me and how she spent all her time and energy giving me opportunities that I apparently did not appreciate, and she wouldn't have stopped probably until bedtime.

Of course, I think, *if Mom were here, I wouldn't have been in Mrs. Carter's office at all.*

That's when I start crying.

My dad sighs. "Andie . . ." but he doesn't seem to know what else to say because that's where he stops.

I bury my face in my hands as the sobs come.

I'm so sure my dad is going to start yelling at me now. Maybe he'll be like all those dads on television who say, "I'll give you something to cry about."

But I feel the car come to a stop, and I look over to see him lean his head against the steering wheel. His body shakes. Then he sits up and turns to face me.

"I messed up so bad, Andie. I didn't know what to do."

Oh no. I'd rather he yell at me than this. I don't know what to do with my dad falling apart in front of me. That's kind of the whole problem.

But my dad is still my dad, after all, and he seems to know the exact right thing to do. He opens his arms and for the second time in less than a week, he folds them around me. This time, we both cry. Snot drips on his shirt, but he doesn't ask me to stop. It takes a while, but eventually, he lets go, and I move back to my seat.

Dad puts the car back in drive and pulls away from the curb, but he doesn't head toward home. He turns right at a stoplight where he should have gone left. Maybe this has something to do with what Mrs. Carter told him.

"Where are we going?" My voice is barely a squeak.

"To get Paige," he says. "I think we need a family meeting."

I've relaxed a tiny bit after my tears, but my body tenses again. I have to tell Paige what I did.

I must make some kind of sound that gets my dad's attention.

"It'll be okay, Andie." His tone doesn't convince me. Maybe he realizes how weak it sounds because he adds, "You know how much she loves you. Besides, I'm the one she's mad at."

Just as I start to think maybe he's right, he adds, "Don't think this lets you off the hook, though, Candy. What you did was stupid, and we're going to talk about it, okay?"

I can't do anything else but nod. Talking about it I can handle. I wonder if I'll be grounded. *Just don't take the journals away.* I need her words. My mom would have known that. And she'd have made me earn them back with good behavior. Here's hoping Dad hasn't developed her punishment-sensing capabilities in her absence.

He gets out of the car, and I watch him buzz his way into the high school. Beads of sweat form at the base of my neck and along my forehead while I wait in the car. Dad turned off the engine, so there's no AC. In the quiet heat, I feel tired—like more than not sleeping well last night tired. What's that expression? Dog tired. Probably less tired than I have a right to feel, given everything that's been happening and the fact that I got up way too early . . . for what?

Paige and Dad walk out, and I watch their body language. He's slow and his eyes are on his feet. She's still standing tall—he must not have told her—and she keeps looking from him to the car.

I'm still in the front seat, so she gets in the back.

"Are you going to tell me what's going on?"

He takes off without answering her.

"You said it's not serious, but it sure feels like a funeral in here."

Bad choice of words. He whips his head around with an eyebrow raised.

Her hands go up in defeat or defense, I'm not sure which. "I'm just saying."

"We'll talk about it when we get home," Dad insists.

And that's the last thing anyone says. I am tempted to reach over and turn on the radio, but I'm afraid he'd slap my hand away. After he pulls in the garage, he orders us both to go sit down in the living room. "I'll be right in."

Paige and I take a seat on the couch. "Do you know what this is about?" she asks.

I nod.

She turns her body to face me. "Tell me."

My breath comes in shaky waves. "I, um, did something stupid."

Her eyebrows knit together, and she puts a hand on my knee. "Are you okay?"

"It's not like that. I mean. Well, you'll see. Just don't hate me, okay?"

"Andie, what are you talking about?"

Thankfully, just then we both hear a door slam and we turn toward the sound. Dad walks into the living room, hauling a big box, one I recognize very well at this point.

"What the hell?" Paige asks.

Dad shoots her a glance. "Watch your mouth."

She rolls her eyes, but she doesn't say anything.

I'm not prepared for this. I don't think any of us is, but it's exactly what we've needed for a year.

My dad calmly explains what I've done so that Paige knows. "So it wasn't Mom's ghost that you and I were experiencing. I think your sister wants us to hear her. Well, we're listening. Is there anything you haven't said that you'd like to add?"

I'm put on the spot, but I deserve it. "I just don't think Mom would have liked what we've become. And when I found the journals, I realized her words are still with us; she told us who we should be, who we are. I don't want us to forget. Paige, she wanted you to have friends and go to college and you've just kind of stopped trying. You both have."

At first, Paige is mad. Really mad. But in the end, she's probably more disappointed than angry. She wanted Mom's ghost to be real. That makes my heart hurt.

Dad shows us all of the things in the box that he kept. We talk about her smells and her journals.

When he pulls out the phone, he turns it around in his hand a few times. Paige is still pretty quiet except for some sniffling.

"You know, I call her sometimes," he says. "It's stupid, but I feel better when I hear her voice on the message and when I tell her what's bothering me."

There's a pause, and finally, in a voice so quiet it takes a second before I realize it's Paige, she says, "I sent a postcard to heaven."

Dad's head snaps in her direction, and we both watch her carefully.

"Just once. About six months ago. I felt like I couldn't breathe if I couldn't talk to her. I was so worried about the house and the bills and Andie, and I was at Walgreens when I saw this rack of cards. I don't know."

Dad reaches out and touches her shoulder. For the first time in over a year, Paige's shoulders relax and she starts to cry. My dad wraps his arms around her and she lets him hug her.

She won't look at me. But then, her hand reaches in my direction, and she touches fingers. It's not much, but it'll do. For now.

Then we get to the more difficult parts. He's got a problem, he says. We already know, but it's important for him to say it out loud and for us to listen.

Epilogue

Gisela and I huddle together in the stands. It's the coldest Homecoming in a decade. I couldn't care less about the game, but Gisela spouts off stats and reminds me when to cheer. I'd probably rather be home or at a movie, but it's high school, and this is what you're supposed to do. Besides, we like to watch Leah cheer. Apparently, she'd always wanted to try out but Becki had told her she wasn't ready. Go figure. Leah was so happy to make the freshman squad even though Becki made junior varsity. Actually, Leah might have been relieved they weren't on the same team.

Isaiah sits on the other side of me. He likes football, so he shushes us whenever we comment on something other than a play, like Leah's hair being cute or the other team having ugly colors.

We're high up in the stands, so from where I sit, I can survey the crowd. Becki is surrounded by new friends. Her head is thrown back in laughter. I look away before she catches me staring. I don't miss the Becki she is today, but sometimes I wonder if she'll ever change back to the one she was before.

For a while I was sure I'd lost Gisela and Leah, too. About a week after the big sit-down with my dad and Paige, Gisela and Leah called me up and asked if we could all meet. When we did, I told them more about what had been going on at home and my project. I apologized to Gisela.

"You could have talked to us sooner," she said. "We would have helped."

"I thought you were sick of me talking about my problems."

"It wasn't like that. At least, not for me. I'm glad you had Isaiah to help you, but it really hurts that you didn't come to me."

"I'm so sorry."

Leah explained that they weren't hanging out with Becki very much anymore because she was too worried about appearance and popularity, and I guess she also kept saying some really bad things about me. When they tried to talk to her about it, she turned on them, too. When convincing them to cut me off didn't work, Becki started ignoring them.

As summer started, I did a good job of keeping my friend worlds separate. I'd go to the pool with Gisela and Leah, and then the next day, Isaiah, Amanda, and I would go see a movie. Amanda really loves action flicks. Isaiah and I like watching her yell at the screen.

Then, one day in July, Gisela asked, "How come Isaiah never comes swimming with us?"

The truth was I'd never invited him, even though we were at the pool almost every day.

At first, it was weird. Maybe more for me than for them. I felt like I was bringing two worlds together, and I feared they would destroy each other or maybe me. Mostly, we still do things separately because we like to do different things, but sometimes, like tonight, we can all hang out together.

Starting high school was scary, but the best part is we could leave some things behind when we left middle school.

No, Isaiah doesn't have this huge group of friends all of a sudden, but he's also not a complete outcast either. Of course, hanging out with Amanda probably helps in that department. I don't think anyone would be brave enough to make fun of him now. Plus, he's got me. Well, us.

I hand Gisela my hot chocolate because she's shivering. Isaiah grabs my hand and rubs it between his. We're not dating, but, well, it's complicated. Everyone thinks of us as a couple and we don't correct them. I don't think we plan to date anyone else, but we're just not ready to think of ourselves as anything other than just . . . us.

After the game, we all head to the diner. Paige is working tonight.

"Let me guess," she says, "chocolate milkshakes all around? I can offer a special two-for-one deal." She winks at me.

We all nod, and Isaiah adds, "Maybe some french fries, too?"

Paige rolls her eyes, but she's smiling as she walks away.

We're the worst table because we leave a mess and not much of a tip, but Paige never complains and she always tells me she likes seeing me have fun. Tonight she does take the ketchup away before Isaiah can use half the bottle though.

"Hey, Andie," she calls out as we're packing up to head out. "I'm going to be late tonight. Study group is meeting up."

Isaiah snorts. "Work and a study group on a Friday night? Careful, Paige, you'll turn into me."

I elbow him, and Paige laughs.

Paige is taking classes at the local community college. It was too late for her to apply anywhere else, but they do have a track team, and she says she's going to join this year. Her old high school coach even says if she does well, she might still get a scholarship somewhere next year. Dad says she doesn't need a scholarship. Apparently, there's always been money put aside for college, and I guess he didn't blow all the insurance money—he just lost contact with life for a while. Being at the casino was an escape. There was nothing there to remind him of Mom or the fact that she isn't here anymore. He had to concentrate to play cards. Plus, once he lost, he kept thinking if he kept playing, he'd win it back. "Your brain starts playing tricks on you when you have an addiction," he says. He keeps going to the meetings so that he can spot the tricks before he acts on them.

Paige will probably move away next year, and I'll miss her like crazy, but it's what she's supposed to do. It's what our mom wanted her to do.

"You'd better get going," she says. "Dad's going to get worried."

Paige didn't talk to me for two days after that day Dad picked me up from school and told her what I'd done. I was so scared she'd never talk to me again. But on day three, she came to my room after her shift at work. I was under the covers, reading, and I didn't hear the door open. She lifted the blanket and slid in underneath.

She glanced at the book I was reading. "Is that one of Mom's?"

I nodded.

"Why are you reading it under here?"

I shrugged. "I don't know. It just feels better . . . safer."

Her eyes narrowed for a second, but then she said, "Will you read it to me?"

We didn't get far that night before we were both crying, but it was a start, and things got better every day after that.

Gisela tugs my arm to pull me out the door. "See you later!" I yell to Paige. She smiles. A big one. I'm so happy my dad was right about her forgiving me.

That's not to say that everything is perfect. I doubt it ever will be, but I guess life never is. Dad has kept his job, but he still has bad days where he can't get out of bed. Some days, I'm the same way. On those days, I like to read—I've reread every journal about a hundred times now. And Paige seems like she's doing better too, now, but when Dad went on a date last month, she ran out of the house, slamming every door behind her and calling him names.

We're still figuring things out. But when things happen now, we talk about them or we fight about them, and then at least they're out in the open.

All those months, I wanted things to be normal again. Nothing will ever be the same as it was before, and I'm sure I'll always wish things could be different, because I can't ever be glad she died. I haven't seen any more signs of her, and yes, I still look. But I feel closer to her now. We talk about her. We remember. In a way, I think I was right, though. I know what I did was wrong and all that, but maybe we needed to believe in her ghost before we could finally stop feeling haunted.

Acknowledgments

As a little girl, I wrote "Be an author" at the top every list of future goals I ever made. So I am gushing with gratitude for the folks who have played such an important part in making this childhood dream come true.

Jennifer Linnan, my literary agent, is my champion. I wonder if she has any clue how stupid I looked jumping up and down and dancing in my office the day I got the email asking to talk about representation. I still do that happy dance, knowing she's the one in my corner, the one who believes in my writing, maybe even more than I do.

As if having an amazing agent isn't enough, the universe blessed me with a meticulous but gentle editor. Fortunately, Adrienne Szpyrka has an attention to detail that I lack but a love for my characters that I appreciate beyond measure.

Thank you to everyone at Sky Pony Press for your commitment to my manuscript and that amazing cover.

This book would not exist without the amazing fan community of a book about sparkly vampires. All those lists as a child, yet I never wrote a single word until my first foray into fandom. Heather, my fabulous frequent cowriter, unwittingly showed me how fun writing could be. Working with her kept me going even though I had no idea what I was doing. And the readers, my goodness, the readers who became friends and unconditional supporters. Stacey, Allison, Lucy, Katie, and Heather S., among countless others, you will always have my heart. BATgirls forever!

My growth as a writer depended on the feedback, critical suggestions, and intense support of a number of folks in various writing communities. Thank you to my Writer's Village University and SCBWI Wisconsin critique groups who read so many of my words, always making them better. Thanks to Jessi for your support and encouragement throughout the long query process.

At its heart, this novel is about family and friends. Not only would this book be incomplete without them, but my whole life's story is only worthwhile because of the people like Jeanne, Darla, and Rachel who are always there when I need them.

I offer heartfelt thanks to my parents who gave me a life of opportunity. My world is full of curiosity and acceptance because of them. I'm able to pursue this dream because they knew when to say "no" and when not to get in my way. It might as well be your names on this cover of this book.

I need to thank my kids for their patience. They put up with a lot of "Hold on a minute; I'm working on something" when I'm trying to write. Sometimes my fiction is bolstered by a few examples from their own lived experiences, so I apologize to them and thank them at the same time. They say publishing a novel is like having a baby. As happy as I am to share this story with the world, nothing gives me more pride or makes me feel more accomplished than being the mom of Grace and Faith.

If you're reading this far, I have a confession: like Andie's mom, I might be just a wee bit of a control freak. No one suffers as a result of my condition more than my dear husband, Bill. Thanks for putting up with my schemes and plans and schedules and novel dreams and just this overall crazy, full life.

About the Author

Tricia Clasen is a college professor of communication. She is coeditor of *Gendered Identities: Critical Readings of Gender in YA and Children's Literature* and the author of several book chapters focused on gender in contemporary young adult fiction. She lives in her much-too-frigid home state of Wisconsin with her husband and two girls, her parents, and what seems like a small zoo. Most of her time is spent shuttling her kids to dance and trying to get the glitter off the kitchen floor as well as planning trips to much warmer destinations.